ESTUARIES

Soeiro Pereira Gomes

TRANSLATED BY TIAGO SILVA

8th House Publishing
Montreal, Canada
www.8thHousePublishing.com

Copyright © Tiago Silva 2025

All Rights Reserved. 8th House Publishing 2025

First Edition

Design by 8th House Publishing

ISBN 978-1-926716-81-7
Set in Garamond & IM FELL

LIBRARY AND ARCHIVES CANADA CATALOGUING IN PUBLICATION

Title: Estuaries / Soeiro Pereira Gomes ; translated by Tiago Silva.
Other titles: Esteiros. English.
Names: Gomes, Soeiro Pereira, 1909-1949, author.
Description: Translation of: Esteiros. | In English, translated from the Portuguese.
Identifiers: Canadiana 20250292106 | ISBN 9781926716817 (softcover)
Subjects: LCGFT: Novels.
Classification: LCC PQ9261.G67 E8813 2025 | DDC 869.3/41—dc23

With support from *DGLAB / Cultura* and *Camões, IP - Portugal*

REPÚBLICA PORTUGUESA
CULTURA
DIREÇÃO-GERAL DO LIVRO, DOS ARQUIVOS E DAS BIBLIOTECAS

CAMÕES
INSTITUTO DA COOPERAÇÃO E DA LÍNGUA
PORTUGAL
MINISTÉRIO DOS NEGÓCIOS ESTRANGEIROS

INTRODUCTION

In translating Soeiro Pereira Gomes's *Esteiros*, I entered a world where poverty robs children of education, play, and hope, forcing them into back-breaking labour and a life on the margins of society. Written in 1941, the novel stands as one of Portugal's most powerful works of social realism, exposing the human cost of industrial modernization through the intertwined lives of a group of young boys. Structured around the four seasons and set against the backdrop of a riverside village and its local tileries—traditional facilities producing tiles and bricks—it follows their daily struggles and the premature erosion of childhood under social and economic pressure.

Yet amid this world of exploitation and hardship, what most stood out to me about the text was the way Pereira Gomes infuses the narrative with passages of lyricism and childlike imagination— fleeting moments of laughter, play, and beauty that sustain a fragile innocence and make its loss all the more acute. These interludes are what I most hope readers will discover through this translation.

Translating for English Readers

Bringing *Esteiros* to English-speaking audiences meant navigating a delicate balance: preserving the emotional force and social urgency of Pereira Gomes's text while ensuring natural readability. Where Portuguese linguistic structures and terms clashed with accessibility, I prioritized clarity and flow while striving to retain the novel's thematic richness.

This principle guided me from the very first step of my work: translating the novel's title itself. Within the text, I consistently rendered *esteiros* as "inlets", the most direct English equivalent. However, for the title, I chose *Estuaries* to better convey the tidal, transitional nature of this landscape to English readers—a place where river meets sea, mirroring the narrative's convergence of traditional ways with industrial change and childhood with the demands of hard labour.

This blurred relationship between fresh and salt water environments appears throughout the novel in the characters' tendency to refer to the river as "the sea"—a feature of local speech patterns and the worldview of Portuguese river workers, for whom this boundary is fluid, both geographically and linguistically. I kept this usage to maintain their intimate relationship with this liminal environment.

One particular challenge involved Pereira Gomes's use of quotation marks to frame characters' inner thoughts while presenting them in the third person. Using the closest English equivalent—italicizing third-person thoughts— risked confusing readers, since italics conventionally signal first-person reflections. Instead, I adapted these passages: some became first-person internal monologues to deepen intimacy, while others were woven into standard narration when a first-person shift would have felt jarring. Though substantial, I judged this intervention necessary to portray the essence of the characters' inner lives in natural, fluid English.

I also sought to capture the authentic voices of the characters by suggesting social distinctions through recognizable English patterns while being careful not to slip into caricature, ensuring dialogue feels genuine yet accessible. Character nicknames like "Gineto" and "Gaitinhas" remain in Portuguese, as their symbolic resonances emerge organically through context. While some nicknames could translate effectively, others resist English equivalents, so I maintained consistency by keeping all in their original form. Other Portuguese terms are likewise kept where translation would compromise their cultural specificity, with endnotes provided for readers seeking deeper insight into these linguistic and historical nuances.

What to Expect

English-speaking readers will encounter a work that feels both historically specific and surprisingly contemporary. While the context of 1940s Portugal may seem distant, the novel's tragic themes continue to resonate, offering a timeless story about children caught between innocence and harsh necessity.

This translation aims to honour what makes *Esteiros* such a compelling work: its raw depiction of social conditions, its deep compassion for the vulnerable, and its recognition that behind every examination of poverty are individual human stories of remarkable complexity. In bringing these Portuguese voices to English, I hope readers will discover not only a masterpiece of social realism, but also a work that illuminates enduring struggles for human dignity.

— Tiago Silva

ESTUARIES

Soeiro Pereira Gomes

To the sons of men who were never children,
I dedicate this book.

CONTENTS

Inlets, slender channels, like the fingers of an outstretched hand, etched into the Tagus riverbanks.

Fingers of the greedy hands of the tileries that steal silt from the waters and vigour from the young crew. Muddy hands that only the river caresses.

AUTUMN

I

THE TILERIES had shut down. With the first signs of autumn, the early rains filled the dark marsh of the inlets with murmurs, and the harsh wind tore holes in the boys' rags, sending shivers through both water and bodies. A desolate gust also whipped across the kilns and machinery, keeping the smoke from rising high. Such an industry needed wind, true; but it needed sun also. Wind to dry, and sun to fire—so decreed the masters.[1] But the sun hung low: it didn't fire the tiles, nor the young flesh of the crew.

More than the weather, it was the poor sales that had the owners refusing to risk more money on the firings. "Bad year…" So they said every year, ever since the French tile had come along. And then the cement blocks made everything go from bad to worse.

"It's a poor industry, Mr. Castro," Zé Vicente would lament as he paid the rent for the land. "A poor industry…" And so it was, from the tattered boys to the ditch diggers who came from afar—seven hours by train, dreaming of impossible wages. That's why the 7th of September went by unnoticed now, without celebration. Once it had been sacred. Wages were paid, debts of three months settled, and farewells celebrated. The boys would spend the last of their energy decorating the tilery, fashioning instruments from tin cans and rattles, and parading around. And as the green reeds of the inlets swayed atop the kilns, the dry canes of fireworks would soar into the sky. Owners and masters would smile with the assurance of conciliation; boys and ditch diggers would sing, yearning for a better life.

Those were the good days! The masters still shouted as before: "Hey, you lot! Move it, this is the last batch." But the rhythm of their step didn't change, for the crew knew they'd pay for their rest with seven months of hardship.

And so the workyards were left deserted. Only at the Big Tilery did a few dozen bricks remain, which the master had ordered to be stored due to the bad weather. Even those would soon be stacked in the sheds, which had good tile roofs and were more voluminous than any of the tilery boys' dwellings.

There lay stored the sweat of a summer of toil. Wind and sun; toil and sweat—that's what the tileries wanted.

✦ ✦ ✦

ON THE LAST Saturday, the boys at the Big Tilery received their wages with shouts of joy. The coins didn't fill the bottom of their pockets, but their young minds were brimming with plans. The next day, the Fair would open; there would be bull parades and bullfights, circuses and merry-go-rounds.

Their excitement was giving the master trouble at payment time.

"If you don't shut up, I'll smack one of you!" he bellowed, as he advanced toward the shed's door.

Silence fell. Those nearest to him backed away in fear. But Gineto[2] promptly shouted from a distance, "You might as well kill us!"

"What for, man? Bones are all he'd get…" Sagui[3] muttered, pointing to his scrawny frame.

"Either you shut up or I'll put an end to this!"

They fell quiet. Missing their pay would mean missing the Fair. And the Fair was the true send-off for the tilery boys. Five days of revelry between a summer of toil drawing to an end and a winter of misery looming ahead.

The payments proceeded.

"Malesso!"[4]

"Here." And as he shook in his hand the money he had received, he exclaimed, "This is for my new suit…"

"It would've been new two years ago, you liar," Gineto sneered.

"We'll see about that tomorrow."

"Sagui!" the master called.

"I'm here."

From the back, one of his companions asked, "You gonna eat all the Fair's cakes with that?"

"If they fit in here…"

He patted his belly, and the boys laughed. Sagui was small, but he had a reputation as a glutton. Just a reputation…

The master continued: "Guedelhas!"[5]

"Here."

The boy walked away with his head down, counting the pay his brothers and his father, who had been unemployed for two months, were counting on. His companions knew about it, so they didn't tease him.

"Gineto!"

Without a word, the boy stepped forward slowly.

"Lucky you, eh!" the master said sarcastically. "You wasted the season this time."

"Only because I like you so much."

Face to face, they glared at each other.

"You loafer…" the master growled.

"Dog!" Gineto shot back. And he darted out, pushing past his mates.

One of them guffawed. "Run, Gineto."

"Run from what, man?" He stopped menacingly. "If he comes at me, I'll fight my way out. What do you think?"

The other boy fell silent with fear, and Gineto went on his way, cursing the master and the tilery.

How many times, in moments of quiet rebellion, had he thought of paying back with interest all the foreman's insults and quitting… He had already done so at every previous tilery. At age seven, his father would drag him by the ears to the workyard. "Master, please take charge of sir high-and-mighty here," his father would say.

But before his father could reach the gate, he'd dart through the inlets' reeds and jump into the river, clothes and all. The current was strong, but the other bank held birds, grazing wild bulls, and yet-to-be-explored embankments. At night, instead of supper, the usual beating awaited him, and the next morning he'd be dragged back to the tilery by his ears.

He lived at the edge of the village, near the inlets. From the house his father had built, all wood and tin, you could see bulls grazing on the other bank and the path of the boats. Clumps of rush and abandoned trash dotted the inlets. But Gineto dreamed of conquering every street. When he was little, he transformed the inlets into forests and searched through the trash for precious toys. But he soon grew bored of that monotonous place, all water and flatland. The forest only reached his waist—it was all just rushes—and the trash was just that, trash. That's when he started sneaking off to the street. His mother would tell him as she closed the door, "Keep an eye on the little one!" But he'd leave his brother crawling in the mud to go harass boys like himself. He wasn't yet Gineto, the *thief.* That name came later with the raids on orchards, forests more beautiful than the inlets. But he was already mean and feared. He sometimes had friends among companions who needed his sure hand to kill loose chickens or to pluck fruit from secluded orchards. Outside of that, he was truly a shunned troublemaker.

This time, however, the Fair enthralled him. He wanted to make up for everything in those five days of revelry, free from the master's commands and his father's beatings. He would watch the circus acrobats; he would fire the cannon and ride the merry-go-rounds. He would even cool his boiling blood inside the stalls with gaudy curtains where painted women sold refreshments and kisses. He would be master of the Fair and of his own fate, free, like a man.

But money was needed, and so he had stayed at the tilery. And, like a man, he had sold his arms so that money would now jingle in his trouser pocket. Gineto felt so happy that he didn't even think about the tears his mother would shed over him and the week's wages.

He walked up Mirante[6] alley, whistling. The estates lay before him, carving up the valleys and seducing the eye. The sun, still high, made the white walls whiter and cast rejuvenating golden glints on the withered vine leaves. But Gineto didn't fear the afternoon light. He was certain the caretakers wouldn't be on watch in the orchards, since the best fruit had already been picked. The tilery boy knew about harvests.

Yet, when he reached the road, he hesitated. For the first time, his estates—his, as he called them—didn't tempt him. The Fair caressed his thoughts; the money jingled in his pocket... He was free, with no caretakers or guard dogs chasing after him... He wouldn't go for the grapes.

And so he continued down the road, savouring the Fair in anticipation. He was a reveler with bare feet and patched trousers, because unlike Malesso and the others, he didn't have a new outfit to debut at the Fair.

II

IN THE MORNINGS, when the factory whistles startled every home, Madalena would lean out her window in Mirante alley.

It was a sad alley that frightened away the sun. It climbed in ledges up the rocky slope lined with walls dressed in mourning and low doors resembling holes. Silent and somber, it had at the top, perched on blackened rocks, an old olive tree that stained the sky's blue with grey. In that alley, life withered.

Madalena would watch her former workmates pass below, waving to her in haste as they continued on their way, lamenting her condition: "She looks so thin!" "Poor thing. She won't make it through the winter."

And she would listen to their whispered voices and remember the time when she too had been a weaver. Then, she would say good morning to her elderly friend, who, with her halting gait, always came late.

"Feeling better?"

"Thank you, Ti[7] Rosa. I might be able to go with you next week."

This she had been saying for a long time, ever since her cough first reddened her handkerchief. But days turned to months—and her improvements were like the winter sun.

If only Pedro would return... she thought. She needed her husband more than she needed sun and medicine. But the former office clerk had been taken to a distant land, which in Madalena's imagination was an inhospitable desert where one dies of thirst and abandonment. He had lost his job and then himself for the sake of that foolish idea of setting up a daycare for the weavers' children, who spent hour upon hour locked inside their homes or tumbling about in the street.

The daycare never came to be; and Madalena was left alone with a child in her arms—the boy who, years later, on a certain autumn morning, went to her to show her his torn boots.

"Mother, look at this. School starts next week…"

She hesitated for a moment, not knowing how to show her son the empty home, the cold hearth…

João insisted, "I can't go to school barefoot, can I?"

"Listen, my son. I am sick, I can't work anymore."

She wrapped the boy in her arms and, looking at his frail body, murmured without conviction, "You're a man now, João. You can help your mother."

Pedro's last letter came to her mind: *"…Send our son to school. Without an education, he'll be either a slave or a vagabond…"*

"So I won't be going to school anymore?" João asked.

"You will, when I get my health back."

The boy grasped the uncertainty in her answer and dropped his head onto his chest. He was about to ask, "Won't I become a doctor?"—But emotion choked his voice.

"Tomorrow," his mother continued, "we'll go talk to Arturinho's[8] father. He will get you a job at the Great Factory."

"A job…" he repeated silently.

Pedro's letter had said: *"When I return, I want to make him a man of worth. I'd like him to be a doctor and to walk into the homes of the poor like a ray of sunshine."* If his father knew that his son wouldn't become a doctor!

For a moment, Madalena recalled the sacrifices made to raise João: days of hunger so he could eat; privations and hardships so he could study. If his father only knew!

João remained silent—the boots forgotten in his hands and his eyes wide open to keep himself from crying. His mother gently stroked his hair.

"You'll earn money and get new boots." And, trying to smile, she promised, "Then you'll go back to school."

Go back... when? the boy wondered. *The others will move up a grade; Arturinho will take his exam and leave school.*

"Maybe Arturinho will lend me some boots," he mumbled timidly. "He's my friend..."

His mother shook her head dejectedly. "And what about money for books and paper? ...You have to understand. I'm very sick."

Eyes meeting, mother and son stared at each other in silence. João was starting to get it. And Madalena reflected: *A slave or a vagabond... Better a slave, because vagabonds lose themselves, but slaves can break free.*

"Come on, you have to be brave," she whispered as she kissed him.

João nodded, head down. And suddenly, unable to hide his tears and despair, he broke free from his mother's arms and raced down Mirante alley, which harboured shadows and scared off the sun...

He wandered the streets like a sleepwalker, fixated on the

idea of speaking to Arturinho, but he didn't find him. Anguish overflowed from his innocent spirit, distorting the small world in which he had lived. Now, he stood at the threshold of another world, full of dangers and hurdles, with no schools and no Arturinhos. He felt fear. A terrible fear of the men he would have to face and the difficulties to overcome. His head ached, and he couldn't coordinate his thoughts. His mother's illness... his torn shoes... he could deal with those. He'd say, "Mr. Joaquim, half soles on my shoes only, please!" At the pharmacy, he'd hand over the prescription while admiring the coloured bottles on the shelves, and the pharmacist would say, "Is the medicine for your mother? Here you go, my boy." But these thoughts still didn't cheer him up. The image of the school was being replaced by the Great Factory's big sheds. He was staring at one, a very dark one, where pale boys darted in, then came out bent and dusty, pushing two-wheeled carts. A fat man also appeared, shouting, "Get to your spot, you lazy dog!" And João didn't take off running as he had the first time he went to the factory. *That* was his school now... He entered. It seemed to him that a huge blackboard blotted everything out. He couldn't see the teacher or Arturinho...

Suddenly, he felt someone tapping his shoulder. He turned around. It was Maquineta,[9] a former classmate.

"Are you going to the Fair, Gaitinhas?"[10]

João didn't answer. As if waking from a deep sleep, he looked around in surprise. Only now did he realize it was night and that he was at the square, under streetlamps pouring intense light over a sea of people in commotion.

As he took in reality, Maquineta leapt onto the back of a

car and shouted, "Come on, buddy. It's free."

Madalena's son watched him until the car vanished around the street corner. He remembered Maquineta had quit school too when he was in second grade. The teacher would call him: "Your turn, Manuel."

"What, Mr. Teacher?"

The rod on his ears explained the question to him, and his classmates laughed, envying the toys he carved with his pocket knife.

"I can't read, but I make stuff," he'd snap back, showing off rough cars and boats made out of wood.

With spite, the others scoffed at his precocious talent, which he trusted more than he trusted books.

"When I work with machines someday…" he'd always swear. And with all that talk of machines, they nicknamed him Maquineta.

João was Gaitinhas because he liked to mimic the music band's instruments. On concert Sundays, he'd take a spot by the bandstand, behind the conductor, his eyes glued on the shiny saxophones and clarinets, torn over which one to pick.

One day, his mother asked him, "What do you want to study, João?"

"Music," he shot back. But once in school, he chose to become a doctor, following his father's wishes from the letters he'd read so many times. Pages filled with old dreams and plans, folded in a trunk like useless relics.

Dejected and aimless, he now stood in the square. Ragged children chased cars and rode them, hiding, crouched atop the bumpers; others, in their Sunday outfits, waited beside their parents for a place on the buses. Every face showed glee over the free hours they would enjoy, forgetting their homes short on bread and the tileries heavy with labour. Only Gaitinhas was sad. He didn't snag a free car ride or mingle with the crowd. He headed home alone, mulling over the world of barefoot and illiterate boys like Maquineta to which he would soon belong.

+ + +

MADALENA and her son climbed the enormous staircase flanked by flowering vines, and Arturinho ran to hug his friend.

"Have you come to play with me?" he asked.

"No. We came to talk to your dad."

"Ask him to see us, will you?" Madalena pleaded.

Arturinho made the request and the door swung open promptly to let the boy's friend through. His papa came out courteously to receive the visitors. However, he neglected to offer them a seat when he noticed that Gaitinhas hadn't wiped his torn boots on the doormat.

Eyes fixed on him, Madalena slowly unwound her rosary of tears and struggles. Her words struggled with the cough in her chest, her hands knotting the faded shawl. *This way, I'll get nowhere*, she thought. She could tell from Mr. Castro's blank face. Or maybe she was mistaken… It might just be the smoke from that awful cigar blurring a welcoming smile on the rich man's lips.

"My son João was in the same class as young Artur. I was

still running odd jobs, but then I got worse... Now he can't take his exam."

"What's wrong with that?" Mr. Castro remarked. "Surely you didn't mean to make him a doctor?"

Madalena lowered her eyes. *What can I say?*

"The teacher said he's very bright..."

Mr. Castro launched into a spiel about too many doctors, the shortage of hands in the fields and workshops, and complicated stuff she couldn't grasp. A coughing fit drowned the words for a moment. *If only I could rest a little on that blue sofa in the corner,* she thought.

Mr. Castro seized the break to check the time—time was money, after all.

"Well then, have your son apprentice in a workshop. If he's as smart as you say, his future's set."

"Yes, Mr. Castro. That's actually why I came to talk to you."

"Go ahead, then."

His tone betrayed impatience. Gaitinhas's mother asked him to pull some strings at the Great Factory and wrapped up: "It would be a huge favour, Mr. Castro."

"But I don't own the factory, woman."

"No, but you have power."

The cigar in the rich man's mouth flared brighter. Power, yes—he had that alright. Famous estates spread across six leagues around, and a name that everyone tipped their hat to. But that's exactly why he didn't like asking for favours. He only took those asked of him. By nature, he had never turned down alms or a desperate plea made to him personally. Zé

Vicente would come every year begging for a reduction on the tilery's rent.

"Mr. Castro, this was such a rough year…"

"We'll see… Yes, rough year, no doubt… We'll see."

"Just a little cut…"

"Well, we'll see."

Once the deadline expired, Zé Vicente would get the final notice to pay the rent.

Madalena pressed her plea too. "If you could do me that favour, Mr. Castro… For your boy's sake."

"So what's the kid's name?"

Madalena gave his name and age. "And when might I hear back, Mr. Castro?"

"We'll see. I'll send word to you later."

Grateful, Gaitinhas's mother bid him a good afternoon and left. Out in the garden, her son had already ridden the tricycle and admired the presents Arturinho got for his twelfth birthday. But he didn't play as he had on other occasions, with restlessness and curiosity, itching to grab everything. After Arturinho asked him when he would return to school, he had felt like a stranger there. He rode the tricycle just because. And when his friend bragged that his daddy would give him a bike if he did well on his exam, João sat on the steps and didn't speak again.

"João, let's go…"

Good thing his mother was calling. He wanted to escape from that annoyingly flowery garden, that house stuffed with furniture and toys, and even from Arturinho, his friend.

"You know what? Mr. Castro promised to get you a job at

the factory."

He accompanied his mother as if he hadn't heard a thing. Then he went and sat at the top of Mirante, overlooking the town.

At times of inexplicable sadness, when the alley's shadows crept into his soul, he'd climb the hillside searching for sun and horizons. And each time, his adventurous eyes discovered new worlds.

At his feet, the village's squat, white-spattered houses looked like toys. Here and there, a tall-gabled residence dominated the borough, propping up the other houses. Dovecotes, Gaitinhas called them, because it was from them that a flock of doves shot out every evening, streaking white across the blue firmament. How often he'd wished he were a dove too! To soar off through that expanse, cross the river stretching lazily over the floodplain like a monstrous snake, and slice the far-off mist with a wingbeat shiver. That colourless veil had to be hiding his father, because he'd always heard that he was far, far away…

Gaitinhas also liked to probe the village when the sun dissolved into colours behind the hills. That's when his alley's shadows walked the streets with the ones coming out of the factories. The doves formed clouds and lost themselves in clouds. And the clothes hanging from windows were flags of peace.

"João, come eat. It's time…" his mother would call. He'd stay a few moments longer. Voices and street cries made into music by the wind would reach him. Then the first star would sparkle in the sky over the village. And Gaitinhas—dizzy with sleep—would blink at the stars.

He loved the village like nobody else. And yet, his childhood had drifted between the alley and Mirante. Only later did he come to know the streets that led him to school. The other boys would be down below playing; but he wouldn't leave his castle of dreams, where he lacked for nothing—like the prince in that beautiful story his mother would tell beside his straw bed...

Now, after he'd left school, everything had changed. The storybook prince he'd pictured himself as got buried on that first day of class, shrouded in the mist that had come from far off, right into the village. And the doves didn't leave their dovecotes—those mansions like Mr. Castro's. And the sun didn't come out that day, or the ones after.

So Gaitinhas decided to head down to the streets. Down there, among that group of boys who looked like ants, had to be Maquineta, his old buddy. He'd carve out his new fate alongside him and the others.

III

THE FAIR was at the edge of the village, right by the road. Three streets flanked by stalls of burlap and unbleached cotton; the circus at one end, the bullring at the other, streets packed with people, stalls crammed with trinkets. The crowd taking their desires for a stroll… The vendors keeping their hopes up…

Over the rough entry arch, a hoarse loudspeaker stubbornly tried to liven up the square with tired music that nobody listened to. The nosy sun laid bare the ugliness of the stalls and the jarring mess of that heap of miseries. By day, the Fair was a joyless camp. "A disgrace to our town," the civilized gents said in the cafés. The young ladies "rightly" sneered at that mishmash. And the old timers reminisced, "Back in the day…" But come night, they all flocked to the Fair. The moon kindly lent silver glints to the burlap and stripes. And if it happened to hide behind clouds, a thousand coloured bulbs were there to fix the faded paintings. At night, the Fair was something else entirely.

That's why Gineto spent the afternoon itching for the lights to come on and, afterward, found the sickly paleness of the girl at the shooting stall more alluring. She was called Rosete, and had strange eyes to match her name. He had picked her out of all the others. She too had noticed that there was a tough guy there, a sort of Tom Mix[11], the kind who'd chase bulls off and take on guards and caretakers without a flinch.

"Fancy a shot, mister?"

He grabbed the rifle, aimed… and missed.

"Bad luck… You'll hit it this time," Rosete insisted with a smile.

Gineto found her voice sweeter than the singing of goldfinches in the fields, despite the shots booming beside them. He continued firing the rifle until Rosete asked, "Will you pay for this one?"

She bent her waist, fragile as a reed, and fired with her back to the target, before Gineto could get a good look at her taut breasts.

Then, embarrassed, the boy decided to practice at another stall.

"I'll be right back."

And he returned at night, but with no money.

"Fancy a shot, mister?"

He didn't want to show he was broke. "Later."

He leaned against the counter with his eyes glued to Rosete, who went on to attend to other customers. One of them, after shattering countless clay mugs, whispered something that made the girl laugh and set Gineto's heart racing. *That's too much!* he thought. He rummaged through his pockets for the last of his wages. *If only I had five tostões…* [12] Disappointed, he decided to end the torment. And when his rival took aim with his back to the target, Gineto tripped him and sent him sprawling across the counter.

Fearing trouble, Rosete calmed the brewing fight.

"Leave the kid be. It was an accident."

"Looks like he's in love with you," another girl jeered.

"Don't be silly! I don't wean babies."

Gineto pushed his way through and fled, seething with shame. He was back to being just a tilery boy, wandering aimlessly through the Fair's streets, catching shoves and taunts.

"Hey, kid! Are you blind?"

Yes. He looked without seeing, because, to him, the Fair was Rosete. At the tilery, when he dug in, not even a beating would make him yield. Now, he faltered. He'd watch her from afar as she doled out smiles to customers. He'd walk away and try to lose himself in the bustle of the other stalls, but he remained blind with passion.

Otherwise, he would have greeted Sagui, who was going from tray to tray, like a gluttonous bee, haggling over the price of *queijadas*.[13] "How much, Ti Maria?" And the deal would be hashed out between his right hand pointing at the cakes and his left clutching the coins.

"Any cakes left, Sagui?" a friend asked him.

"The sesame cakes are running low. But if you're paying, I'll put away the tarts too…"

He sometimes thought about his squandered wages and the lean winter coming in. But his enormous mouth would quickly reveal his gluttonous teeth, his mischievous eyes competing with the flies on the trays of sweets.

The rest of the Fair was for the others. For Maquineta, who was determined to figure out the carousel's workings, and for Guedelhas, who strolled through the streets with empty pockets, having handed his earnings to his unemployed father. As for Malesso, he had chosen the ring-toss stall, until he managed to loop one around a Port bottle—top-shelf stuff, judging by the label with gold lettering and red flowers. Then, after downing the wine, his squinting eyes could only focus on the top of the ramp, where the torpedo was supposed to hit. But that thing weighed more than the rings. Malesso persisted, refusing to give up, while the machine's owner rubbed his hands with glee.

"That didn't count," he'd say after each failed attempt. By then, his shirttail had ruined the neatness of his suit, and the tie knot, which had taken so much work, had slipped off his collar. Clutching the torpedo, he was losing steam.

"Eight... Nine..." the stallholder counted, tallying up the supper he'd bring his wife and kids late that night, after the Fair's streets emptied out. And Malesso grumbled, "That didn't count."

Eventually, an impatient hick complained, "Looks like you rented this for the whole night..."

The stallholder heard and tapped Malesso on the shoulder. "You owe four *mil-réis*[14] already..."

"I owe nothin'. I haven't even lit the lamp."

That's how the ruckus started. The stallholder's yells drew a curious crowd that encircled the contenders. Drunk and sweaty, Malesso wanted to leave.

"It didn't count. Let me go..." But the stallholder's hands didn't care about the new suit.

"One way or another, you have to pay."

"I'm not payin'!"

The hicks grinned as they egged on the fight, and Gineto joined in, adding to the chorus. Then, someone shouted,

"Here come the guards!"

Spurred by those words reminding him of the farm guards, Gineto seized the confusion and dragged Malesso into the nearest stall, where they hid.

It was a dark stall on the tavern street. "Swallows' Restaurant," the garish sign said. Grimy tables and benches on a dirt floor; cheap cretonne curtains covering the booths at the back; and a huge frying pan for *miombas*,[15] amid parsley sprigs and fish slabs. A foul, sticky odour seemed to ooze from the old cook and the other women waiting for customers at the counter.

But Malesso stirred up the stall. "Wine! I want wine!" The women came to fill the glasses and flash their rotten teeth. Gineto didn't even feel the warmth of their ample, brushing breasts.

"Malesso, let's go."

"Let me be…"

A swearword finished the sentence. Gineto was tempted to smack him, but decided to leave him instead. At the door, he made it a point to warn the women: "Watch out, that guy hasn't got any money."

"Hasn't got… hasn't got…" Malesso repeated with a slurred voice. He rummaged his pockets and showed a hand with a few coins.

"Four *mil-réis*," counted one of the women, who then eyed the empty tables and waiting booths. Four *mil-réis*… He would be her first that night. And she leaned against the boy.

✦ ✦ ✦

GAITINHAS spotted Gineto right at the entrance to the Fair. Before, he wouldn't have spoken to him. But now, having left school, he saw himself as his equal.

"Gineto…"

"Hey! Are you here to buy a clarinet?"

"Your dad wants to beat you. He just got here."

"What's it to you?"

"Nothing. I came to warn you."

The answer threw Gineto off, and he asked, now in a friendly tone, "Who told you that?"

"I heard it myself on the road. He said you ran off with your pay two days ago and that he's going to thrash you."

"Don't sweat it, my dad won't catch me." And then he suggested a carousel ride.

"But I don't have any money…"

"I'll pay."

They stopped by the carousels—there were two of them. The bigger one, lit up with multi-coloured bulbs, caught the eye. It had horses with hooves in the air which looked as spirited as flesh-and-blood steeds; roosters with tall crests; various animals on a rolling platform that swayed like boats on the river. The other one, rickety and dim, just had horses.

"Which one you want?" Gineto asked.

Gaitinhas took his time to answer. He looked at the old carousel, with no one on it, and the sad, still horses. The owner's hoarse voice seemed to call him. "It's gonna run… It's gonna run…"

"Let's go on this one," said Gaitinhas.

Gineto handed over the ten *tostões* Sagui had lent him so he could buy another smile from Rosete. The lights flared with brightness; the bell announced the ride and drew more people.

"It's gonna run..." And it did, to the worn-out hurdy-gurdy tune of the rumbling, panting motor, as a pale man tried banging cymbals in time.

"Sweet tune," Gaitinhas burst out.

Maybe it was the music from the big carousel drowning everything out. But whichever one it was coming from, it was beautiful. It made him forget his mother's illness and his busted shoes. The horse galloped through space, across the stars, and he carried a smile on his lips and his exam pass to show his father...

In his mind, Gineto became Tom Mix, digging spurs into the horse he'd named Malacara[16]. With his teeth clenched and his kerchief billowing in the wind, he held the pale Rosete in his arms, having snatched her from bandits. The horse vaulted over walls and inlets without stopping. And Malesso, Sagui, and all his buddies from the tilery waved from far, far away...

The carousel stopped. But the joy of the ride still danced in Gineto's eyes and on Gaitinhas's lips.

"Thanks, pal," said the latter.

"Now let's go check stuff out."

Gaitinhas was taking a shortcut to the shooting stalls, but Gineto didn't want to go because he had no money left. They headed to the trinkets and crockery street, which was always packed with people. Gineto's parents were there too, going from place to place, hovering around the stalls.

"That little jug, Manel..."[17]

"You're crazy."

"I just wanna look…"

"It sticks to your hands like glue."

"When I get a job," Deolinda's boyfriend dreamed as he whispered in her ear, "I'll buy you earrings like those."

As the crowd went from place to place, hovering around the stalls, their eyes bought everything. Gaitinhas stopped too, eyeing the harmonicas, spellbound, just as he would be at the bandstand on concert days.

"Want one?" Gineto asked.

"You bet I do! Even if just to try it out."

"Then ask the guy to show you that doll…"

"Which one?"

"The one at the very top."

Gaitinhas did as told. The man began saying it cost fifteen *mil-réis,* but before he could even grab it, Gineto's hand had already swiped a harmonica. A few steps away, he handed the prize to his friend, who was dumbfounded.

"You stole it?"

"Of course…"

Gaitinhas didn't want to accept it. He remembered his teacher's lectures in class: *"Whoever steals deserves exemplary punishment…"*

"Don't be silly," Gineto went on. "One more or less… Who cares?" And he added as an excuse: "If I had the money, I'd buy it."

Gaitinhas tucked the harmonica away, mulling over what he'd tell his mom. Then he realized it was time to head home.

"I'm off, Gineto."

"It's still early, pal. Come grab some cakes."

They found Sagui chatting with Guedelhas at one of the food stalls.

"Wanna hit the cakes?" Gineto pitched.

The others nodded, and they picked their target in a clearing among the crowd.

"Who's going first?"

"Me," Guedelhas said.

He walked with his hands in his pockets, feigning nonchalance. Then, he shoved a tray with his body and bolted.

"Ah! You rotten devil!" the woman yelled, running after him. "If I catch you... you scoundrel!"

Sagui and Gineto stuffed their pockets by the handful, and the former even mocked, "Grab that rascal, Ti Maria!"

From a distance, Gaitinhas laughed at the mischief. He only felt bad when he saw the woman's gutted face.

"Poor woman!" he said to the others. "That's not right."

His friends shrugged their shoulders. "We're hungry..." Sagui was always hungry. Gaitinhas's stomach, which had been empty since morning, demanded its share too. After splitting the cakes, the group scattered, and Gaitinhas headed home with Guedelhas.

"Where have you been, João? Is this the hour to come for supper?"

"I went to the Fair with Arturinho."

"Did you talk to him about the job?"

Caught off guard by the question, he dodged: "Tomorrow..." And he handed his mom the cakes he hadn't eaten.

Gineto and Sagui were still at the Fair, biding time for thieving, when the stallholders would be nodding off from sleep and weariness. But the rain came, deep in the night, soaking the streets and stalls. Near the cart where the two boys hunkered down, someone groaned, "Even the ground's no good for a bed now." A child cried. "Shut it!" shouted the same voice. "This damn rain's bad enough." Silence returned, broken only by the downpour on the awnings. Then, a woman's pained voice: "You didn't even bring me soup…"

"Was I supposed to steal it? I told you, the boy ran off without paying."

Gineto thought of the torpedo man.

"Now what?" the woman pressed.

"We hitch the donkey, and that's that."

Far off, beyond the floodplain, patches of light lifted the mist. The rain had stopped. And in the fairgrounds, here and there, tired arms were taking down the tents.

IV

NOVEMBER 1st. All Saints' Day and the day of "God's bread". Children spread out through the streets and knock on doors. "Bread… in the name of God…"

There are walnuts, chestnuts, and dried figs stored away in chests… Tradition demands the children not be turned away with mere words of patience. The poor scrape bread from their own mouths to give it to the children of the poor. And the rich shake off crumbs, in the name of God.

All Saints' Day—the day of all the poor.

✦ ✦ ✦

SAGUI BARELY slept the night. Through the thatched roof of the hut that had once belonged to the vineyard watchman, he saw the stars shivering from sleepiness or cold. Most certainly from sleepiness, because according to his theory, as soon as the sun announced the day, they closed their eyes.

"Gineto, I figured out that the stars sleep during the day."

"You're nuts."

Even though he was mocked, Sagui stuck to his claim. He looked up to Gineto, who had a solution for everything; but when it came to stars, he really knew nothing at all.

"Then why can't we see 'em now?"

No one had an explanation. Coca,[18] who lamented not

being able to read, piped up, "If I'd gone to school, I'd know."

Days later, Sagui asked the same question to a fourth-grader, and when the boy clammed up too, he became convinced from then on that the stars slept during the day. He loved them, Sagui did. He'd even get sad when one streaked across the sky and vanished forever in a trail of light.

But it wasn't because of the stars that he spent the night wide awake. It was because, as soon as dawn broke, he would go begging for "God's bread". Bread which would turn out to be a handful of walnuts, pears, and chestnuts... Anxiety had chased away his sleep and made the hut's floor harder. Beside him, the small bag for the offerings tormented him—under the caress of his hand, Sagui had sized it up and found it too small. He wasn't counting on his shirt, because it was torn and its pockets weren't deep... Through the hole-riddled roof, the stars seemed to laugh at his distress. He tried to sleep. How hard that floor was! The stars laughed again and again... and so did his pals, because they had gotten up earlier and were already halfway through the village...

But it was only a dream. Sagui reached Mirante even before Gaitinhas, who lived only a few steps away but feared raising his mother's suspicions. The other members of the group showed up only later. Sagui trembled with impatience. "It's late, man."

"The whistles haven't blown yet," observed Malesso, his eyes all crusty.

In front of the village, like generals planning an offensive, the boys coordinated how they'd spread out for the assault

"What about Gineto?" one of them called to mind.

"He's not here… Let him sort himself out."

At eight o'clock, they set off. Other kids—skinny and covered in rags—emerged in pairs from the houses, forming a legion in the streets. In the dull serenity of the morning, their languid voices carried the tone of a sacred chant.

"Bread… in the name of God." From far off, like an echo: "… in the name of God."

Slowly, the voices merged into one anguished cry that drowned out the last words.

"Bread…"

Sagui was getting desperate. "Say it some other way, Maquineta."

As if he knew how. The voice was no longer his own. It was the voice of all the children who, at that hour, were going door to door in the streets of every town and village.

"What's there to know, man?" his friends rebuked. "You just beg like the poor do."

"I've never begged before…" Gaitinhas bemoaned, not getting the hang of it either.

Oh, if his mother knew he was out there! He, who according to his father's wishes was supposed to become a doctor, knocking on doors like a beggar.

Near Mr. Castro's garden, Coca, who begged every other day of the year anyway, whined, "A little alms, young sir…"

"Mama says she only gives on Saturdays."

"See what you did, you fool?" Malesso whispered. Then he fixed it, modulating his voice, "Bread, in the name of God. Everyone gives today."

Behind the gate, Gaitinhas, red with shame, peeked at the

garden he'd never play in again, a shadow of sadness clouding his eyes. Meanwhile, Arturinho reappeared at the top of the stairs.

"Hey! Catch this." And with a smile, he tossed down, one by one, a few walnuts that the boys scooped up from the ground.

"How many?" asked Coca, who hadn't bent down because he was lame.

"Seven."

"Aw, damn! If today were Saturday…"

Then Maquineta went back. "Hey, kid! This walnut's a dud." And he chucked a rock at Arturinho, who was left crying.

Street by street, the litany continued at doors that had knockers and bells. Because at those that didn't have them, bread was scarce and the residents were out earning it. Accosted as well, Mr. Castro shooed them off the sidewalk: "Go work, you're big enough."

The boys stood still and silent, watching him walk away. *Go work…* easy for him to say. The tileries had been shut down for over a month, and as for work, promises were all the boys could find. If his friend Gineto were there—Gaitinhas thought—he might cuss out Mr. Castro right to his face. But Gineto hadn't wanted to beg for God's bread and was now out stealing from one and the other, and throwing rocks at everyone.

"Gineto, don't swipe my figs, they're for my grandma," Pirica[19] pleaded.

"Your grandma's old, she's eaten loads."

"Gineto…"

"Let go, or I'll smack you."

When the boys roamed in a pack, he'd hide around a corner and chuck rocks at them. Then, once they scattered, he'd corner them one by one.

"Split it with me quick. And shut it, you hear?"

It was on one of these runs that Gaitinhas found him.

"Leave the boy alone."

"Buzz off, Gaitinhas…"

"If you let him go, I'll give you these walnuts and figs."

Gineto stopped and stared at him in bewilderment. No one had ever shared with him like that, with no resentment. And for the second time, Gaitinhas defused his meanness. First at the Fair, when he warned him his dad was set to whack him; and now, here…

"Thanks," he muttered, letting the other kid go.

The two of them climbed Mirante's hillside and sat down at the top.

"Take some figs," Gaitinhas offered.

"I've got my own."

"Then why were you stealing?"

"Beats me."

Gineto didn't want to confess that he didn't beg because people chased him away from their doorsteps, calling him a thief and a bum. He'd never forget the thrashing he'd gotten a year before at the hands of Mr. Castro. He had boldly walked into the garden: "Bread, in the name of God…"

"Here you go, boy…" And the blows left marks on his body, all just because he'd pelted rocks at the caretaker when he'd gone to raid the High Farm.

Maybe that cowardly, late punishment was why he was now chasing off the more fortunate boys.

"Gaitinhas, are you my friend?"

"I sure am."

Gineto smiled. He'd never had a friend like that. He knew well that the others sucked up to him out of fear. Except for Sagui, everyone cursed him, even if they respected him.

Gaitinhas pulled the harmonica from his pocket and started playing a popular tune, which his buddy listened to in a trance. He didn't know anything about music, but that song was surely the most beautiful in the world. It erased the scars Arturinho's father had left on his body and soul, carrying him to friendly arms he'd never known before.

"That's amazing, man!" was all he could say when Gaitinhas finished.

Night was slowly creeping down the slope of Mirante. And with it, a good feeling was dawning in Gineto's chest. The afternoon's quietness called for secrets. They shared them. Like old friends, they laid out the story of their short lives— lives with no history. Gaitinhas confessed the pain of quitting school due to his mother falling ill.

"What about your dad?" Gineto asked.

Madalena's son looked at the mist shadowing the horizon. "He's very far away," he murmured. Then, fearfully, as if revealing a crime, he added, "He wanted me to be a doctor."

Gaitinhas's voice was all crystallized tears. And Gineto felt bad that being a doctor wasn't something he could steal.

On the watery road of the Tagus, boats were gliding gently. Gaitinhas wished he were a boatman so he could take a boat to the port where his father had ended up. Gineto noticed the boats too, but griped, "One of these days, I'm heading to sea. My dad already said he'd tie me to the boat…"

"I'd like to go."

"Well, I'll do it only if I can't find a way to escape."

"And then what?"

"I'll figure it out."

They fell silent. Boats, doves, and the sunset—the whole landscape of that late afternoon poured into Gaitinhas's eyes, leaving him in awe. Gineto, however, only saw the long inlets of the tileries, like fingers clawing at the waters—those and the slender factory chimneys, which the twilight darkened even more.

"Shall we go?"

They said goodbye to each other. The doves returned to their nests, and the two friends did too. Meanwhile, on the river road, the boats continued gliding, seeking a port for shelter or work.

✦ ✦ ✦

IN THE HOLE-RIDDLED hut that had once belonged to the vineyard watchman, Sagui smiled at the stars, his friends. He had laid down at his side the small bag that the offerings hadn't filled, and slept. His shallow pockets hadn't been needed, but it had been a day of plenty. He had only been turned away by that old lady who had forgotten about All Saints' Day, the day of all the poor.

Sagui had knocked at the door again and again.

"Have patience," the lady had snapped.

"Bread, in the name of God…"

"I already told you!"

Then, Sagui had stuck out his tongue and yelled, "My belly's full of patience already, you miser!"

Still not satisfied, the old woman came back, deep into the night, stretching her crooked fingers toward the offerings bag. So ugly was she that the stars shivered with fear, and Sagui's heart pounded so hard that he woke up startled…

Then he smiled at the stars and drifted off to a sleep without nightmares.

V

A COLD AND FOGGY dawn at the end of autumn, foretelling a winter full of rain and hunger.

Maria do Bote[20] got up, tiptoeing so as not to wake the children. She opened the shutter to see if dawn was breaking over the fields across the river. But the night was as dark as a poor man's life. A drizzle was falling.

"I wonder what time it is," she muttered. "I could sure use an alarm clock."

It was a dream she'd had for years—owning a clock to wake her at set times, like a dutiful maid in a rich folk's house. *Someday I'll ask Costa Ourives[21] to sell me one on instalments. I might manage to set aside two or three mil-réis per week,* she thought. She did the math—tallying things was a daily affair.

Meanwhile, she placed the pot of soup leftover from the previous evening over the fire. The clay brazier warmed the hovel's air and spilled faint light across the packed-dirt floor, while the furniture skulked in the shadows. In one corner, sagging from generations of use, stood the iron bed where the couple and their baby girl slept; at the center of the house was the pine table that Manuel do Bote had cobbled together; in another corner, separated by the worm-eaten dresser awaiting the trousseau, lay Deolinda's and the boys' straw beds.

Manuel do Bote got up too. "Got the coffee hot?" he asked his wife in a low voice.

"Coffee? Not even dregs."

"Damn this luck!" And he went out the door, heading straight for the inlet—that dumping ground for trash and slop. Then he laid his eyes on the boat and let them drift downriver. It had to be time. The high tide would hit around five, and the water was already licking the tip of the inlet, caressing it tentatively. Manuel do Bote splashed his weathered face with water and returned to the shack.

"Chico…"[22] he shook his sleeping son."Hey, boy!"

An otherworldly groan answered him. "Yessir…"

"Get up. Did you hear me?"

Gineto rubbed the darkness from his eyes with slack hands, still clinging to sleep. He hovered for a moment on the bridge that leads night into day. A tall, dark figure before him seemed to him the caretaker from the High Farm. Was he still dreaming? But his father's hoarse voice snapped him awake for good.

"Hop out of the nest, I'm in a hurry. It's time."

Time for what? he felt like asking. His bulging eyes stared at the shadows swirling on the floor as he yanked on his pants without even realizing it. *What does my dad want with me?* Ominous feelings were taking hold of him. In bed, his brother slumped against his back. He shoved him off and the boy started whimpering.

"Shh…" his mother hushed from the corner.

His brother fell silent, and the quiet grew heavier. *Why's he calling me this early?* Suddenly, it was as if a blindfold had been pulled from his eyes, like when he played blind man's buff. He saw it clearly now—he was bound for the boat.

"Dad…" The sound barely escaped his lips. *What would*

I even I say? No, I won't beg just to be refused. With a rough, phony air, he edged toward the fire. His mother handed him the reheated soup, and he ate. Then, he grabbed his brimless cap, tossed the bag of supplies his father handed him over his shoulder, and followed him without saying a word.

The inlets' dewy sedge creaked under his groggy steps. Out there, the boat looked like a ghost ship from some movie. And Sagui's stars twinkled in the sky, like fireflies on an August night. *Lucky Sagui. Sleeping soundly, doing whatever the hell he pleases… While I'm here, at this dead hour, barely awake, on my way to a cage.* The cold froze his body and his will.

"Grab the oars to warm up," his father ordered.

Gineto dropped the supplies, sat, and the skiff began sliding smoothly toward the boat, though his defeated arms lacked skill and spirit. The oars scraped against the tholepins, wounding the water and the silence—they groaned in his stead… Finally, they docked. The boy set foot on the boat, but his gaze remained distant, seeking lost freedom. Except for his eyes, his whole being was trapped.

"You asleep on your feet? Hoist the sail!"

On the ghost ship, his father was the captain. *Where's he taking me? Back to the city, like that other time?*

It wasn't long before the wind puffed up the sails and the crew's shirts, and the sun came splashing onto the river. The boat pulled up to the dock with a skillful maneuver.

"Hey, Gineto!"

He saw Malesso laughing by the edge of the dock.

"You off to Africa, man?"

He acted like he hadn't heard and kept pulling at the rope.

The other boy shut up. But Gineto, on the sly, could still see the mocking grin plastered on that misshapen face. If he weren't trapped there, he'd have beaten the smirk out of him already. Instead, he waited for his father to ask for the mooring line, then flung it at Malesso, who lost his footing and tumbled face-first into the mud. Gineto's howling laughter filled the dock.

"Ti Manel..." the other boy complained from below. But Gineto's father was laughing also.

Then the factory sirens drowned out the laughter, setting the village and the dock in motion.

Maria do Bote, who hadn't slept a wink since her husband had gotten up, fearing she'd be late to the looms, shut the door on her little ones and left with Deolinda. *If only I had that alarm clock...* She returned to that sweet thought, the same one she always had whenever her husband left home with the stars still out, or when her weary body craved rest. *But this time, I won't just stand in the street hovering over Costa Ourives's window...*

After gulping a shot of *aguardente*[23] at the tavern, the stevedores shuffled toward the dock. Their eyes still longed for bed; their quiet mouths puffed out boozy breaths; and work bags dangled from their hands. They looked tired. But when the siren made its final call, they immediately stretched their muscles and grew larger. Woe to the man who couldn't keep a brisk pace under a hundred-kilo sack! For the back-and-forth never stopped—couldn't stop—from granary to boats, from boats to granary.

The *Boa Sorte*[24] was one of the first to take on cargo.

The men of land and sea performed feats of balance on the gangplank and eased their backs against the gunwale.

"Hi, Gineto…"

They greeted Manuel do Bote's son, who was busting his ass in the boat's hold, stowing the wheat.

"No more grapes, huh?"

The men of land and sea teased and laughed; they still had laughs and teases left in them. *Boa Sorte's* new shipmate was the only one who'd lost it all, even his strength. Him, a tough guy like the cowboys, unable to budge a tumbled sack. Panting and sweating, he bit his lips, but wouldn't cry.

"Come on, tough guy!" Malesso's father piped up.

"Harder than climbin' trees, huh?"

More than his father's glares, it was the men's talk that kept him there. Twice he'd thought of escaping—and given up. He dug into the pride of being a man among men… And he bit his lips… And the boat's hold was a bottomless pit…

"It's like the boss's belly," someone quipped. Now the teasing was thinning out, and so was their strength. The breath from their downtrodden chests no longer stank of booze—sweat was pouring off the dock.

"Keep it movin'! Let's go…" But the men of land and sea were men like any others.

"Takes time, the bastard…" one said, panting. And like this man, many others anxiously awaited the loading of the precious cargo.

Finally, the *Boa Sorte* set off. Stuffed to the brim with wheat and fatigue, its half-sunk hull was pushed downriver by the wind. From bilge to sails, the whole thing had swollen up.

Gineto had already collapsed from exhaustion onto the sacks—sacks that still had to be covered with tarps. The weather wasn't looking good, his father had said. He craved sleep… To wipe out the sight of men buckling under the yoke of God knows what, and of his own body too. To sleep, to dream of *his* estates and the open streets where his friends played. Now, he lacked even the courage to escape. The village had faded from his eyes, and the tileries were slowly vanishing. He could still make out the tips of the inlets, like fingers of gnarled hands— hands that didn't reach for him in the deep of autumn. In the distance, hills piled atop hills touched the sky. But Gineto no longer looked at the sky, like he did as a child, when he'd climb to the peaks to press his hand against the blue dome.

On the river's back, the boat was no longer a ghost ship— it felt like a cradle being rocked. Only the captain remained unchanged, gripping the helm, his face hard and his eyes sharp.

"What about the tarps? If the wheat gets wet…"

Now that he'd closed his eyes and fancied himself a child in a fantasy cradle… his father had to come remind him of a crewman's duties. He threw the last of his strength into the work and, as if that weren't enough, sudden downpours soaked his shirt and riled up the river.

"We're in for rough waters," predicted the captain, who knew everything. He'd steered the boat's keel close to shore, dodging reefs and wind gusts. Gineto helped reinforce the sails. For the rocking didn't lull him anymore—it scared him—and the river was now a restless sea. The afternoon light gradually dissolved in the rain. All around, everything was hazy. From far away came the whistle of a passing train, its lights dragging, leaving darkness behind. More darkness and longing for Gineto, who followed it with his eyes. *If only I could be on it... At this hour, my friends are probably in a doorway somewhere, telling stories.*

"Are you hungry?" his father asked.

He said yes and went down to the cabin, from where he took out bread and fried horse mackerel. They ate. Gineto also took a sip of wine that his father offered him, and cheered up when he heard him say, "We're close. We'll be in Lisbon before the day's out."

They got there at night, at the time when a host of stars seemed to Gineto to have fallen upon the illuminated city. He fell asleep, down in the bottom of the boat, thinking of wonders. And in the morning, he wanted to unravel the mystery of the sunlit streets that were buzzing with people. Women—and how beautiful they were! If only they could see him chase off a bull...

"Dad, aren't we gettin' off the boat?"

"You crazy?"

He got it into his head that he'd find Rosete among those women. His father pulled him back to reality. "Cut the nonsense. Let's get to it."

He felt like lunging at the man, who wouldn't even let him dream. But the unloading began. The crane stretched out its huge jointed arm and immediately lightened the boat by hundreds of kilos. Gineto felt lighter too—no stevedores' jabs to bother him, and the work was easier. Even so, he worked up a sweat. So much so that his father, who was always stingy when it came to displays of affection, patted him on the back, smiling. "If you keep this up, you'll score a new suit next month."

He could hardly believe his ears.

"A new suit?!"

"Yes, son."

As if he were already wearing it, he jumped, whistled, and even forgot about Rosete. *The boys will be green with envy when they find out. If only I could get back quick! On one of those steamers with smokestacks as thick as pines that rumble louder than the factory whistle.*

Even heading back on the small boat didn't dampen his joy. He waved goodbye to the crewmen of a boat that passed on its way downriver; he looked fondly at the barren hills, no promising estates in sight; and, like the river's surface, he felt the sun's warmth on his back.

When he jumped ashore, he ran straight to the town store… The blue suit he'd been passionately eyeing before the Fair was gone; but he'd pick another one, he figured. Then he went around the streets, spreading the news.

"Hey, Malesso! Did you know I'm getting a new outfit?"

He didn't even remember his rival's fall in the mud at the dock. Malesso didn't say a word to him. The other boys, likewise indifferent, were chasing tipcat sticks or flicking marbles. To them, Gineto wasn't a street kid anymore, he was no longer a playmate or tilery buddy. He'd grown up. A crewman on a boat, he now belonged to the class of men who walk into taverns and toss cigarette butts on the floor. Cigarette butts that only they, the kids, would salvage. And Gineto had left them without warning. He had knocked Malesso down out of spite, and gone off.

Now, newly-returned Gineto grabbed the tipcat stick that had landed at his feet and asked, "Can I play?"

"No."

"Oh, I can't, huh? Watch this." And he threw the stick onto a roof. The others hurled all the dirty words they'd learned in the filthiest streets at him, and Gineto challenged the group: "One at a time. Come at me…" He puffed out his chest, clenched his fists, and planted his feet waiting for his opponents. But only Sagui stepped forward, his scrawny frame shielding him.

"You're a piece of crap. Muscle's all you got." And face to face, he dared him: "Go ahead and hit me. Hit me…"

Gineto stood like a statue; then, having been defeated, he threatened Malesso: "You're the one who's gonna pay for this. You've been spreading rumours…"

He turned his back on the group and walked down the street, feeling abandoned and sad. He'd gone there with friendly intentions—and lost his friends. And to think he'd spent the whole way back from the river itching to share his news! He was getting a new suit; but he wouldn't be envied like Malesso and the others had been, back at the Fair.

At the street corner, he stopped in indecision. Against his will, he'd traded the streets he'd ruled for the sea, which belonged to no one. And now he found himself alone, a dethroned king, searching for a fate. *What if I went into the tavern? Dad gave me ten* tostões… *Maybe I can sell the two pocketknives I have left from the Fair.* He went in.

At that late afternoon hour, the poor men's club was

packed with people: factory workers with faces as hard as machine steel; sailors who carried the river's unrest in their eyes; herculean stevedores with childlike laughter; here and there, men with slumped arms, waiting…

They were celebrating the night, which brought them rest and oblivion in the folds of its black coat. The night was their day. Some sat at grimy tables, seeking in card games the luck that work denied them; others drained glasses of wine, regaining strength—or the illusion of strength. For everything there was illusion: a jumble of laughter and voices; an indefinable melody in the music pouring from the radio; and in the smoke-filled air, floating on top of it all, a vague dream of happiness…

Gineto approached the counter. "Don't push, boy!" someone in front of him rasped. He stopped, hand mid-air.

"A glass of red!" he shouted. His voice got lost in the murmur of the crowd. He made his way around the counter and tried to break through the wall of bodies.

"Ti Manel…"

"Wait!"

A shove pushed him back. He was about to give up when someone grabbed him by the arm.

"Look who it is, the little rascal…"

The Dock Warden bared his foul mouth in a wide grin. Gineto shuddered. He'd fled from those hands so many times, and now here he was, caught like a rat.

"Come for the melons, have you?"

Gineto couldn't remember which melons stolen by the water's edge the Dock Warden was referring to. All he could think about was how to get away quickly, with all his might. *If only I were closer to the exit...*"

The Dock Warden was dragging him toward the counter. "Come here. Want a drink?" And his laughter reeked of *aguardente.*

"You scared? Come on..." His chubby hand fell lightly on the boy's neck, flushing his face—more from shame than the hit. He tried to break loose before more laughter could erupt from the mouths around him.

"Let me go! What did I ever do to you?" His voice betrayed what his mind and muscles wanted.

"You don't remember?"

Yes, now he remembered. He had run away from home and the tilery, gone hungry, and stolen melons from a boat. Then, while being chased along the dock and the river, he'd made the Dock Warden take a forced bath.

"You shameless thief..." The Dock Warden couldn't see the boy's burning cheeks. He kept insulting and hitting him.

That's when Gineto remembered the pocketknives. With his right hand free, he felt for the blade and, in a sudden jerk, stabbed it into the arm holding him.

✦ ✦ ✦

DRIVEN OUT and hunted like an animal—Gineto by name and condition. A street kid who'd strayed from the streets and didn't grow into a man, because he'd fled from men. Better to live like Sagui, without home or hearth. To sleep in a hayloft open to the stars and beg for "bread in the name of God". To be good and cheerful. No, he couldn't be good. Sagui had lost his parents but gained friends, while *he* would always be an orphan in the world.

Forsaken and now more sorrowful, he sees an ambush at every corner, an enemy in every shadow. That's why he runs. He climbs the slope of Mirante and stops for a moment, remembering the encounter he had there with Gaitinhas one afternoon, when the boy had declared himself his friend. He had turned out to be a false friend like the others, who had believed Malesso's gossip. There are no friends for someone who's hunted like a beast in an open field... And yet, he hadn't wanted to be a beast. It was against his will that he'd tossed the tipcat stick onto the roof and drew the pocketknife in the tavern. Why had they scorned him when he, happier and calmer than ever, was going to get a new suit? Why? No, he couldn't be good.

In the moonless night, no one came to brighten Gineto's darkness. And he kept sinking into the night that augured evil thoughts. Around him, the trees' shadows looked like giants and winged creatures. A dog barked in the distance and the sound echoed through the ravines, giving voice to the creatures and giants. Gineto opened his eyes to the night and shuddered. He was near the High Farm, between the walls of vineyards and orchards on which his hands had left their mark. The shadows were no longer of giants and creatures, but of caretakers and guards. And the barking was getting closer... And Mr. Castro's shadow moved, stealthily, like on an autumn day—a day of "God's Bread"...

Frightened, he turned back. He even thought about going home, taking his chances. But on the dock, the red light of the beacon outlined the boats' silhouettes. A light that guided lost sailors to safe harbour. That's why he, a sailor for a day, went down to the dock. The prison he'd hated days before now turned into a soothing refuge. There was the *Boa Sorte*, looking like a child's cradle in the serene waters. In the moonless night, the beacon was the only star... And the boat kept rocking, rocking...

Gineto, the child, entered it and slept.

WINTER

I

THEIR HANDS forgotten in their pockets and their feet purple from cold, the boys pressed themselves against doorways, waiting for soup or for the sun that hardly warmed anything. Once kings of the streets, they had now abandoned them in the onslaught of water and wind, having been beaten in an unfair fight... And so vanished the imaginary world they used to play in.

The wind swept from side to side in a mad rampage; it rattled doors and windows, and left everything desolate and bare, like the trees in the valley. Then came the rain, turning the river—a narrow stream of dark water in a ditch—into a sea of mud that flooded the streets. There were sunken boats, crumbled castles, wilted gardens... Works of art, once feats of fancy, were lost in the deluge. Where the steep, rocky slope of a hill once stood, there was now a mysterious lagoon where faces with restless, sorrowful eyes looked back at themselves.

Pressed against doorways, waiting for soup and for spring...

"Sagui, tell us a story."

"Not now."

Stories were told on summer nights, while the kilns licked at the kindling. There'd be stars in the sky, the moonlit tilery becoming a surreal stage. Back then, the boys would get spellbound hearing about princes, and they'd live the stories that Sagui told better than any scholar: "Once upon a time there was a prince…"

Now there were no princes, no stars.

"One of these days I'll start at the factory…" Maquineta began to dream aloud.

"Sure you will."

"I put in a request…"

Everyone had put in requests at the Great Factory. A hope passed down from parents to children, from generation to generation. Gaitinhas remembered Mr. Castro, to whom he'd also made a request, and Malesso complained, "Well, my dad wants me to go work in the fields."

"And are you going?"

"What? No way… Sleeping with the oxen and plowing from sunup to sundown… They say they even beat you there."

"Better to take a beating and eat than go hungry," Sagui remarked. "We get beaten at the tilery, too."

"Are you crazy? You don't even earn enough for a bite of food there. And if you get sick, nobody takes care of you. How can you think that?"

The other boy didn't answer, and Malesso let his thoughts carry him on a tormenting journey to the countryside. With a bag on his back and credit-bought boots on his captive feet, he crosses the river and disappears from the world, into the endless floodplain. He steps into a huge, gloomy shed. "Ti

Manel…" He has no idea if the guy next to him is even named Manuel.

"No one knows who you are out there…" Malesso concluded out loud.

"I wouldn't mind either way."

Sagui knew the world. He'd begged for alms from town to town, while the others had only begged door to door on the days of "God's Bread". He knew the world, except his own hometown. And he never found his parents, no matter how far he wandered.

"I've got a lot of faith…" Maquineta replied. So did the others. Only a disheartened Coca said he'd go begging, even as Sagui insisted there was already too much poverty around.

"Whatever. I'll say I'm crippled…" And he showed his shaky, feeble leg.

Silence returned, broken only by the chattering of teeth against teeth. Malesso sought warmth from the butt of an expensive cigarette he'd forgotten in his pocket.

"Give me a drag," pleaded Guedelhas, who'd been quiet until now.

"It was hard to come by. I chased this down like a dog."

Resigned, Guedelhas went back to thinking about where he could get socks to make a rag ball.

"If I had a ball," he murmured, "we could at least warm up."

"Bring wool and I'll make one," Maquineta offered. "I once had one that felt like rubber."

"I can't even get socks, let alone wool."

"You got any, Gaitinhas?"

"Not currently."

"Maybe your dad does, Malesso…"

"He doesn't wear any. Only when he goes bullfighting, but those are borrowed."

"Women's stockings… Now *that* would warm us up," Sagui snickered.

The conversation then veered off to made-up flings with women—Malesso's specialty. Even Coca, who'd pretended not to care about the ball, forgot his limp leg and prattled away like a man. And Gaitinhas learned things school had never taught him. Then, the rain clawed at their half-naked flesh and froze the conversation.

In the doorway, waiting for soup, only dreams staved off hunger. Guedelhas had gone back to the playing field, where there were leather and rubber balls and a big crowd cheering him on. Sagui imagined himself a grocery clerk—at the big store in the square—more intent on eating than serving customers. And Malesso—tight pants, wide-brimmed hat— was riding on horseback among herds of bulls.

"When I become a landowner…"

"You? Liar!"

"Is that so hard to believe?! Castro owns farms galore, and he worked at the tilery too. That's what my dad says."

"Ah, but he…"

"What? Isn't he made of the same stuff?"

"Get real. Try plowing first…"

Sulking, Malesso didn't share the rest of his hopes.

"If only the vineyards still had grapes…"

"They say the persimmons at Poisada are ripe already,"

Coca informed them.

"Yeah, right!"

"Gineto would know for sure."

"He landed himself a cushy gig." And Malesso added, "The guy runs away whenever he sees me."

"It was the Dock Warden he was running from. If his dad hadn't stepped in…"

"What did he do?" asked an intrigued Gaitinhas.

Malesso described the brawl at the tavern and Gineto's arrest, and how his father got him out after a whole lot of begging. And he laughed as he said the Dock Warden had found him curled up like a rat in the boat.

"If it were you, you'd have soiled yourself," Maquineta mocked.

"You're stickin' up for the guy, huh? I don't go around stabbing people."

"You do what you can to get out of trouble," said Gaitinhas without conviction, as he looked at the harmonica Gineto had given him.

"Play us a *fadinho*,"[25] Coca asked.

He obliged, and the others joined in with an off-key chorus, chasing away the cold. But suddenly, a woman opened the door behind them.

"I don't want any noise. Get out of here."

"What's the harm?" Sagui shot back. "Even the doorways don't give shelter anymore."

The woman saw the boys' angry faces and explained, "It's just that my son is very sick."

They left, and the door closed behind them like the lid

of a tomb. But the woman's voice—more sorrowful than the wind—still lingered outside. To shake it off, Maquineta suggested they play matchbox lids. It was the go-to game in winter, when soccer balls were scarce and the rain cooled their enthusiasm. Gaitinhas didn't want to play. The woman's voice had cut into his chest like a double-edged knife; it reminded him of his own sick, shivering mother.

The other boys flicked matchbox lids against the wall. "Tops or bottoms?"

"Tops," Maquineta guessed.

"I won. You owe me two *tostões* already."

"I'll pay you when I start at the factory."

Malesso shrugged. "I'll never get the money…"

"You'll see."

Maquineta's dream had taken deep roots that the winter's grip couldn't shake.

IN MADALENA'S home, winter had already settled in months before. But only now did the dampness begin to drip down the walls and had the dust taken over the shelves.

She'd taken to bed. The hollow in her chest longed for medicine and sun—the sun that never reached the alley. The doctor came one day, thanks to Rosa Coxa's[26] stubborn insistence on a visit. He examined her lungs, pursed his lips, and then, pencil in hand, glanced around the cramped hovel. All around, in that atmosphere of lack as distressing as Pedro's portrait on the bare wall, only Madalena's face was white as snow.

"Please don't mind the mess, doctor…"

He was used to seeing lack of all kinds. He pointed to the portrait. "Is that your husband?"

The sick woman nodded and told him of Pedro's whereabouts.

"I already know." He nodded, then pondered, "If he'd had any sense…"

But he immediately held back his reproach. He too, as a student, had dreamed up grand plans, stood up for principles. *"Life is the struggle for ideals…" "Medicine should be a calling…"* Later, the ideals turned into a struggle for his own survival in that provincial town of humble folks, and the plans—priced by his colleagues—ended up tacked on the door of his doctor's office.

"It's fate…" was all he added.

Madalena pressed her lips together. She knew full well that fate was the will of men.

"All right. Take this medicine with meals. Are you with Montepio?"[27]

"Not anymore, doctor. I fell behind on my dues…"

"Well, I'll come back if needed."

He left, and the small room seemed to get colder.

"João, go to the pharmacy and get this filled. Tell them I'll pay later."

Her son went and came back in a flash.

"Well?"

"I was told they can't sell it on credit, that the medicine's expensive."

With vacant eyes, Madalena began rolling the prescription between her waxen hands. João sat on the chest. Outside, the other boys were playing and laughing—he'd seen them, but chose to stay home so that his mother might break the silence that weighed on everything, even on his father's face in the portrait across from him. He was still and quiet, waiting for something—he didn't know what. Around the house, winter tightened its days-long siege; and on the hearthstone, the ashes were the remains of a lost fight.

"João..." The sound halted on her lips. *Where would my son find firewood? Only by stealing it from the hills.* She pulled the meager bedding tighter around her body. *I wonder what time it is. If only Ti Rosa would come...* The silence—brother to the darkness and cold—persisted. And the hours were the same as any other hour, for the day was an endless night there.

"Did you hear the siren?"

João didn't understand. He was concerned with the harmonica deal—Malesso was supposed to buy it. *Five mil-réis, at least. Five...? Might be enough for the medicine,* he thought.

"João..."

He approached the bed. His mother was still rolling the paper, as if trying to hold onto a last shred of hope.

"Go to Ti Rosa's house and ask her to lend me a handful of coal."

I need to grab the prescription, Gaitinhas thought. "Do you want me to go back to the pharmacy?" he asked, eyes fixed on the paper.

"What for?"

"I'll be back, Mom."

He took the prescription from her hands and ran out looking for Malesso, whom he found down by the dock.

"Do you still want to buy this?"

The other boy wasn't interested in the deal anymore, but he tested the instrument's sound.

"How much?"

"You make an offer…"

"I'll give you… fifteen *tostões.*"

Gaitinhas couldn't believe it. "That's it?!"

"What, you expectin' a fortune?"

"Five *mil-réis.*"

"You think I'm a fool, man? Go pound sand…"

Gaitinhas walked away slowly, with hanging hands and desolate eyes. Then, at Ti Rosa's door, he delivered the message and waited.

"Did the doctor go to your house?"

When the boy nodded, she asked further, "And didn't he prescribe anything?"

Gaitinhas showed her the slip, and she stared at it as if she could read; then she tucked it in the pocket of her apron.

"Here's the coal. And tell your mother I'll drop by later."

On his way home, Gaitinhas played a cheerful tune on the instrument Malesso had snubbed. Ti Rosa would get the prescription filled; and the coal would burn away the darkness—sister to the cold and silence.

✦ ✦ ✦

ALONE AT HOME while her mother wove threads at the factory, she'd fallen from bed and ended up lame. That was ages ago. Nicknamed Rosa Coxa, she'd grown old at the loom, like her mother, who'd passed away.

At the first siren call, she'd already be up in a flurry. With things always running late and the fire refusing to catch… Limping along—firm step, shaky step—she'd fill the house with sighs and commotion. And her house was far from the factory at the edge of the village. With the fire lit and the pot on top of it, she'd shut the door in a frenzy. Then, limping along, down the street that seemed to never end, she'd reach the factory having lost a quarter-hour of pay or with a penalty hanging over her.

"Here comes Rosa Coxa!"

"With her hurry, she doesn't even seem to limp."

She'd hear jeers at the factory and jeers in the street. That was ages ago, before her body took on the shapely form of a woman, which, even so, no man had wanted to marry. Rosa, a rose—but lame… And in her ruddy face, a look of distress that drew amusement.

One day, Madalena offered her arm and helped her along the way. And from then on, Rosa Coxa had a daughter as caring as the one she'd conceived in her maiden dreams.

That's why at the pharmacy, she pulled the unfilled prescription from her apron.

"Fill this, and I'll pay on Saturday. How much is it?"

"Eighteen *escudos*."[28]

"Almost a week's wages…" But she brought the medicine to Madalena as if she were bringing her weekly pay home on a Saturday afternoon.

"Are you feeling better?" she asked from the doorway.

The sick woman gave an unsure nod.

"Turns out your son didn't explain himself at the pharmacy. Here's the medicine."

"How can I ever repay you for so many favours, Ti Rosa?"

"Me? You owe me nothing, my child."

"I know I do. As if the eggs yesterday weren't enough, or the coal earlier…"

"Don't mention it. You get well, and we'll settle up later."

"Well… Ti Rosa, I'm hanging by a thread."

"Talk sense, girl! What couldn't I complain of, an old hag like me?"

She began reeling off examples of other sick women, stumbling over her words like someone reciting a prayer. But only the fire in the corner offered any promise of comfort. Everything else froze in the shadows, like Madalena's smile on her colourless lips.

"Come spring… you'll see," Rosa Coxa insisted.

With her eyes tangled in the portrait, the sick woman remembered the tree that Pedro had planted in their old garden. Each winter more bare, more withered, and always waiting for spring to bring it new sap and blossoms. So it was with her too. She coughed, and the white of her cheeks turned red for a moment. It was a deep cough that wracked her chest.

"Take the medicine," her friend urged.

Rosa Coxa bustled about, trying to tidy up the shabby

furniture. Disheartened that her words brought no cheer, she sought to help with her hands instead. But only the fire, with its pale flickers, offered some comfort there. Gaitinhas settled beside it too—the soup was taking its time. He looked like he was dozing.

"Are you hungry?" his mother asked.

"No, ma'am."

He was lying. With only a mouthful since morning, he was both hungry and sleepy.

In a faint voice, Rosa Coxa spoke to his mother about him: that she shouldn't count on Mr. Castro's promises. A tight-fisted man... He couldn't care less about other people. Especially considering who the boy's father was...

"But what can I do?" lamented Madalena, who no longer reacted as she used to.

"He should go beg for alms if he has to."

"Beg for alms? Oh, Ti Rosa..."

"What's the matter? Shame is for stealing."

She couldn't see the sorrow written on Madalena's face. She'd always disagreed with the idea of the boy going to school instead of learning a trade.

"His mother's sick... so he goes begging. Others who have no need of it are out there knocking at people's doors."

It was worse going through life being scorned, limping along, earning her daily bread—which was always hard-won and tasted of hopeless sorrow. This she thought, but only repeated, "Shame is for stealing, girl."

Madalena kept quiet. She rested her clouded eyes on the portrait, as if her whole life were in that gaze, and silently told her husband what Rosa Coxa could never understand.

II

AT THE DOCK, masts stripped of sails, the boats slumber. The river's empty. For nearly a week, rain's been falling in bursts as thick as the ropes mooring the boats.

"At this rate, Ti Manel…"

"It spells hunger."

"It might ease up. The wind's starting to shift…"

"The wind's like us. It straightens up just as quickly as it twists."

"Twisting's all it does, man. Sea folk always have their bow under water."

"They say a hell of a flood is coming from upstream. There'll be misery by the bellyful."

"That's all we get full of. As for the rest, we're emptier than a pot with no bottom."

At the dock, arms hanging limp, the men wait. The river is a restless sea of yearnings. Words leave their mouths, but the river's the focus of their eyes—the eyes of animals that always forgive their master.

"If I could, I'd change course," said Manuel do Bote.

But those are words meant for the river to hear. He hangs around the dock, a forgotten cigarette butt on his lips, hands dragging like an amphibian's.

"What if we got our throats wet? As things stand…"

Some go. They sit on the grimy benches and drink.

Cards pass from hand to hand, and glasses go from hands to mouths, loosening tongues. But the tavern sits at the edge of the dock—and the river's watching from just outside the door. Chico Lindinho can belt out every *fado* in the book, but it's the river they hear.

Manuel do Bote steps into his boat. He adjusts the tarps, loosens the ropes—as if he were about to set sail. Just like Guedelhas's father, who roams the streets like a man with a purpose, even though he's unemployed.

✦ ✦ ✦

MANUEL DO BOTE'S wife blocked him at the door to their house, her mouth wide with laughter and a package in her hands.

"Guess what I've got here."

Manuel do Bote shrugged at the mystery.

"Beats me. Beef?"

Her laughter dimmed. "What an idea!" She opened the package and placed the nickel-plated clock on the dresser. "Look. Isn't it beautiful?"

Even after setting it in a better spot, she moved it once more. Then she stood back to admire it from a distance, like a devotee before an altar.

"Do you like it, Manel?"

He didn't answer straight away. The clock filled the entire house with its shine—it looked like the beacon down at the dock. But that image reminded him of the empty boat moored at the edge of the sailless river.

"What good's that to me?" he said through his teeth. "Is that supposed to wake me up at noon?"

"For heaven's sake, Manel! Winter doesn't last forever."

"For us, it never ends."

She turned her back on him in a huff. So much scrimping and sacrifice, only to hear that in the end! Weeks and weeks living for that clock, as if a child were about to be born. She felt like asking where he thought the three *mil-réis* she'd been slipping to Costa Ourives every Saturday had come from. But she held her tongue. Manuel do Bote demanded respect; he ruled both house and boat with a firm hand. Now he was pacing from corner to corner, poking here, rummaging there—he was restless.

"The oilskin suit… Where is it?"

"No clue. You took it this morning."

"Goddammit!"

On the boat, everything was in order—he knew where he kept his things… Here… even the air was scarce. Fed up, he sat by the fire, stewing in his gripes. Another week of idle hands, of not knowing what to do, and Lopes from the shop would be knocking at his door to collect the rest of the bill. He should've skipped the repairs, just as he'd been advised by Ti Bento, who knew everything about the ways of the sea.

"It'll still hold through the winter, Manel…"

"That's what you say."

He'd been right. But then again, who could've predicted three straight years of floods and storms like no one had ever seen? He hadn't believed it, and now the boat sat on display at the dock.

"If I could, I'd still change course."

Now these weren't words meant for the river to hear—it was the despair of not being heard.

His youngest son curled up at his legs, whimpering, after his mother gave him the slap she'd meant for Deolinda, whom she'd been scolding. But the soup came to the table, and the scolding ended with their hungry mouths. The clock's ticking became music to Maria do Bote's ears, giving the reheated soup a better taste. Deolinda listened to the rain rattling on the bare ceiling, thinking that surely her boyfriend wouldn't be coming to chat at her window that night.

"What cursed weather!" she muttered.

Manuel do Bote looked up at his daughter—she'd read his thoughts—and he, too, grumbled, "This way, even supper's no nourishment."

A gust of wind shook the tranquility in the house. It was Gineto, bursting in soaked and out of breath.

"Do you know what time it is? Sir high-and-mighty…" his father rasped.

Maria do Bote gazed at the clock hands with delight. "Eight-ten…"

"You couldn't care less about the boat. You think the work's over?"

The boy didn't answer. His father was venting because the boat was rusting and he didn't know what to do on land. Not so with Gineto. He'd become a sailor on the promise of a new suit, but he'd had enough. The suit he'd picked out had vanished from the shop window—it had been replaced again and again—while his own was hanging on a line and succumbing to the cold.

"Is it raining hard, Chico?" his sister whispered.

He nodded without taking his eyes off his plate. His father kept up the tirade, letting out the high tide of grievances that was suffocating him.

"The Dock Warden won't forgive you. You pull another stunt, and I won't be the one to get you out of jail."

I don't care, Gineto thought. The boat's hold was a prison too, only worse—it meant forced labour for life. That's why he'd gone back to "his" estates. He wasn't about to spend the winter watching the dock like his father, waiting for jobs that wouldn't even buy him a suit, while the oranges ripened in the orchards. No, sailors knew nothing of that business.

His father left in a foul mood, and Deolinda went to the window to listen to the drip of water from the eaves that mimicked her boyfriend's footsteps.

"Go wash the dishes, girl!"

"I will. It's still early."

"It's nine o'clock."

Maria do Bote had placed the alarm clock on the table, closer to the bed. She'd almost kissed it when she wiped the fingerprints off with her breath, and now, while she rocked her cranky baby daughter, she watched the big hand rotate with steadfast obedience.

Lying on his back on his straw bed, Gineto was fleshing out his plan from the night before. He'd start with the High Farm, since he knew it well, even though it was riskier, as the caretaker guarded it like a loyal dog—perhaps better.

Cunningly, he even kept the wall close to the house free of glass shards.[29] *The big brute!...* Sure of himself, Gineto smiled and turned his thoughts to selling the oranges. *I need someone who won't raise suspicion. Sagui... Maybe Gaitinhas.* And he fell asleep as he mentally reviewed his entourage of friends.

Meanwhile, his mother wound the alarm clock, just as Costa Ourives had taught her, and blew out the lamp. Deolinda lingered at the window.

"Go to bed," Maria do Bote shouted. "Otherwise, come morning, there's no dragging you out."

Her daughter didn't answer. She'd stopped hearing the drip from the eaves and was happily offering her bosom to her boyfriend's hands.

At dawn, the clock woke the whole house.

"Shut that racket up!" growled Manuel do Bote, who'd come home late for fear of the floods.

The children woke up with a start, and the youngest burst into tears. Only his wife heard the clock as if in a sweet dream—her dream of many years. That's why she let it wind down to the end, despite her husband's complaints.

"Don't you hear that? If I get up, I'll smash that thing."

"The hell you will," she snapped, swinging her feet out of bed. "Maybe you don't want me going to the factory? You rich now?"

Manuel do Bote lay there, watching the light seeping through the disjointed roof tiles. *Even my wife's calling me out for doing nothing, like it's my fault. Someday she might even accuse me of living off her. No, this isn't a way to live. I'll take the boat to a work port, whatever it takes, even if I have to point the bow straight into the flood and through the drowned fields.*

And without a word, he got up too.

THE FLOODS filled the peasants' eyes with tears. Its banks gone, the river had become a sea—a sea of affliction.

But up at Mirante's lookout, overlooking Gaitinhas's house, the folks who came in from the city in automobiles saw neither anguish nor eyes brimming with water. They aimed their binoculars at the floodplain, and the lenses brought close the roofs of submerged houses, collapsed sheds, and the slender crowns of poplars that looked like a drowning man's fingers. Far away in the distance, inside the cut-off chapel, the Lady of Alcamé must surely have been crying out to Heaven.

"What a magnificent spectacle!"

"And you didn't want to come…"

"Will the water keep rising?" someone asked.

A local man from the area nodded. "The crest won't hit until the day after tomorrow…"

The chapel's upper tower could be seen. And the bell— silent, powerless…

"I'd like to come back when the river's even higher," confessed a lady who'd heard the man's reply.

Her husband disagreed. "It's not worth it. The view is striking, but monotonous…"

A flock of wild ducks stirred their gaze, forming a cloud that stretched out and vanished into the morning mist. Along the embankment, once a riverbank and now a path to nowhere, the glaucous crowns of a row of olive trees emerged from the water.

"Look," a young voice said, "those olive trees look like they're floating. And over there, a small house, half under water... It's sad, isn't it?"

"That depends..." a thin and elegant young man replied. "As Amiel[30] said, the landscape is a state of the soul."

"Oh, you see everything through a poet's eyes."

"And why wouldn't I? The blue of the river is now missing, but we still have the blue of the sky, you see? And come spring, joy will return to the sown fields."

Then, turning to his companions, he asked, "By the way, did you read Silveira's article? I thought his explanation of how the floods enrich the soil was quite clever. It's only a pity that his style is so weak..."

The river's muddy current dragged along bales of straw, animals, and tears. And the local man, oblivious to the chatter, saw nothing but mourning before him.

The honk of a car echoed over the village. Some people were leaving, others arriving.

Now it was a fat gentleman, with a camera slung over his shoulder, who was taking in the view.

"Where's the marvel, then?"

"It's grand, you must admit."

"Well, my friend, this is a mere lake, when compared to the floods I saw in America. Now *that* was something. Whole villages wiped out, utterly devastated fields, hundreds dead..."

His friend cut the digression short. "In any case, the

damages run to thousands of *contos*…"[31]

"Yes, I'll grant you that—it's a blow for an agriculture as poor as ours."

"Meneses de Sá, poor guy, is losing over seven hundred *contos*. There's even talk that he's selling his mansion in Estoril."[32]

The fat man fell silent for a moment. A white-sailed boat appeared alongside the embankment, evoking a shroud. The wild ducks skimmed the water and seemed to land on a shapeless log that was tumbling down with the current. But the fat man saw neither the log nor the boat. He was thinking about saving his property-owning friend from the floods—by buying his mansion.

"Poor Meneses! Seven hundred *contos*…"

"The State ought to help him," the other man explained. "There's talk of a big landowners' meeting."

Beside them, indifferent to the city people, other men spoke slowly about the floods.

"They say that upriver—can't recall where—seventy houses collapsed."

"Shacks, probably…"

"No, proper houses. The water got to gnawin' at the clay walls…"

"And what happens now?"

The man telling the story shrugged; the others looked out at the flooded fields. And because they didn't have binoculars, they saw no beauty in the landscape. The river was a grave for their hopes also.

"My brother lost his clothes, his hoe… everything. Came

back from the fields empty-handed."

"At least he made it out in one piece…"

"What for? His wife's already out beggin' with the kids…"

A female voice rang out with excitement. "Look, Mama! Three oxen on that little patch of land!"

The binoculars ravaged the horizon. "And no one's trying to save them?"

"It's impossible," someone explained.

The elderly lady was overcome with sadness and returned to the car. Coca, who had just climbed the hill, tried to plead as she passed. "A little alms…" But the car sped away, and Coca didn't get to tell the city folks that he was lame and that his father had lost everything in the floods.

The fat gentleman had also left the lookout, after tossing away the end of a cigar that Sagui picked up to sell to Malesso. The boy had come to the hilltop hoping to see the tileries flattened by the flood. As it turned out, the kilns were still standing, like fortresses in the middle of a desert. The wind had carried away tiles and coverings; the rain had crumbled bricks; the water had flooded clay pits and mud grounds. But the tileries withstood the weather. Their submerged inlets, like fingers, clawed at the river—gathering silt stolen from the floodplain.

Only Sagui kept the same belief. "Third time's the charm. This year, it'll all be wiped out! Gaitinhas, come see the flood!"

"No need. It's here already…"

The torrent cascaded down the hillside, splashing into the alley. But the water didn't wash away the sadness from the bare walls. From her bed, Madalena had lamented, "The water's gotten in, João. Plug up those holes."

He'd sealed the door, and now, soaked to the bone, he was digging a deep ditch along the rocky slope. But the torrent dodged the path that Gaitinhas had dug for it, and it dragged stones and trash until it spread out into the street below.

"Sagui… Hey! Help me out here."

"Forget it. By the time you're done, it'll be summer."

He took pity, though. "If you could get some bricks…"

"Would stones work? I don't have bricks."

"There's plenty at the tileries."

Gaitinhas smiled. "Yeah, but they've got an owner."

"The owner's us—we're the ones who make 'em. Wanna come? With ten or so, I'll seal your door in no time."

"No. I won't steal!"

Sagui let out a laugh. "Such a choir boy! You won't talk like that once you're working at the tileries."

And he went down the alley, with the dead stub of the cigar in his mouth.

Gaitinhas fell silent and, without a gesture, let the water erode the clay at the foot of the door. "*Once you're working at the tileries…*" *Will I really go?* Everything told him he would: the sunless alley, the blackened walls, and the seemingly never-ending torrent. At home, his mother lay ill; and in the chest, the letters from his father were growing ever more faded.

With tears in his eyes and water up to his knees, he ran through the streets looking for someone to help seal up the door. The only place he didn't go to was the station, where Maquineta and others were offering their backs to the gentlemen arriving on the train from Lisbon.

"I'll carry you home on piggyback…"

"You can't get through. The streets got about a metre of water."

"More than two, actually," Guedelhas claimed.

Coca snickered on the sly and pleaded for alms. "I lost everything in the flood, sir…"

"Everything? Like what?"

He'd start thinking of things he didn't have—and he'd lose the alms.

Pirica, who was stronger than the others, found himself a customer: a pot-bellied fellow brandishing a leather briefcase like a whip.

"This reminds me of donkey races," the man said, roaring with laughter.

"Mind you, I live far away," another man warned Guedelhas.

"No problem, I can manage."

But when he got to the square, his legs were shaking like reeds. "I gotta set you down, sir…"

"And have me get wet? No way—hold on."

The boy took two more steps, wobbled, and they both tumbled into the water.

"You damn fool!" the man shouted threateningly, while Guedelhas slipped away laughing, despite not getting paid the five *tostões*.

His father, who'd seen him, told him to look after his siblings and then waded through the flood with the hurried manner of someone with a purpose. With a saw in hand and a pencil behind his ear, he was going door to door to offer his services. "Need any boards sawed? Need any help?"

Gaitinhas had initially let him walk away, but then, hesitantly, he approached him. "If you could come to my house, sir… I'm friends with your son…"

"Sure, I'll go," the carpenter cut in. "That's what I'm here for. I've got four kids of my own…"

But as he looked at Gaitinhas—just a child himself—he fell silent.

The floodwater had reached the ends of the blanket Madalena used to keep warm. They had to plug up the holes in the door with wood slats given by the neighbours and then drain the room, which ended up thick with mud anyway. Finally, Guedelhas's father said that everything was sealed.

"Do you need anything else?" And he fixed his gentle, watery eyes on Madalena, like an ox waiting for its feed.

"Thank you, sir… I don't even know your name."

"Joaquim."

"I'd like to pay you, Mr. Joaquim, but…"

He tucked the pencil behind his ear to mask his disappointment and replied that it wasn't necessary. He left. And in the street, he resumed that same hurry of someone who has steady work.

"Is it still raining hard?" Madalena asked her son.

"No, ma'am. Looks like the sun's coming out."

He was lying, for it was always night in that alley. Nevertheless, Madalena perked up, as if the sun might yet bring her a cure. The worse she got, the more she held on to hope. "In the spring…" she'd say. She clung to the earth like those decrepit trees that sprout new shoots just before they die.

Sometimes, she even made plans. And Rosa Coxa, hearing her, would weep for her.

Ti Rosa came every Saturday. With a worried face and a bag in her hand, she'd make the rounds at the looms, begging for alms for Madalena, who'd worked at the factory and was now sick with tuberculosis. All the women gave something.

At first, the sick woman had refused. She had cried. "Ti Rosa, I'm ashamed. They earn so little..." Later, she gave in.

"So, feeling better?" the old woman would ask, out of habit.

"I didn't cough as much today. Looks like I'll be back on my feet come spring, Ti Rosa."

And she'd break off the conversation to hide a red sputum in her handkerchief.

✦ ✦ ✦

GINETO'S FATHER said to him, "Come on. We're going after salvage."

The boy happily hopped onto the skiff, wanting to row it by himself.

"Drop that, boy," his father snapped. "The sea's not in the mood for games."

He sat down across from him. The oars creaked in the tholepins, and the wind hissed across the waves that pitched the boat upward. The current dragged it downstream, and Manuel do Bote threw every muscle into the rowing, pitting conscious effort against the brute force of the waters. One broken oar and the skiff would be swept downriver, like the tree trunk drifting nearby.

"Careful, Dad. Watch out for that log."

A hard swerve, and the boat dodged aside. Gineto grinned. He enjoyed being aboard like this, amid dangers. A life where life itself was on the line, and full of the unexpected—different from the one he'd led when the river was a smooth sea.

Manuel do Bote watched the log float off. "So much firewood lost..." he muttered.

"Can't we catch it, Dad? With a big boat..."

Manuel do Bote's face darkened. The big boat sat rusting at the dock, alongside many others, with the sad look of something abandoned: sails down and masts pointing up at the unreachable sky, no starlight shining.

"Get the grapple," the rower ordered.

They were in the middle of the river now. On both sides of the boat, oranges, remnants of shacks, and swollen-bellied rabbits floated by amid scattered clumps of reed.

"So many oranges, Dad! I'll fish them out."

"There's time for that. Do what I tell you."

Gineto had remembered his business prospect. Out here, there were no walls or caretakers... But a strange shape was rolling in from a distance.

"We've got work," Manuel do Bote said. "Pull it out of the current."

The grapple scraped against the empty gasoline drum and locked onto its belly.

"Pull, boy!"

His father didn't need to say it. Legs braced against the

gunwale and hands like pincers on the grapple's rope, Gineto's shins hurt, and he clenched his teeth; but the river gradually gave way in the struggle. The drum bumped against the boat, and the two mariners hauled it up by sheer arm strength.

"Good job!" Manuel do Bote remarked.

Gineto smiled with pride, wiping the sweat off his forehead with his shirtsleeve. His eyes surveyed the distant dock, where people without boats were collecting salvage that the current washed up. Beyond the houses, at Mirante's lookout, others were stepping out of shiny cars to gaze at the river. *They must've seen me,* the boy thought. And he puffed up his chest, as if the fat gentleman's camera were right in front of him.

"Can I grab the oranges now?"

His father nodded while estimating how much the salvage was worth. Hurriedly, as if the High Farm caretaker were coming, Gineto set about collecting the fruit.

"You're gonna tumble overboard…"

He eased his rush. "If I could grab it all in one swoop, I'd dive right in."

His father hid a smile. "I'd have to pull you out like that drum…"

"Think I can't do it?!" And he yanked his shirttail out of his pants.

His father's hoarse voice stopped him short. "You crazy, boy? I didn't come here to fool around."

Other debris from the wrecks drifted closer. The groan of the oars grew louder in the river's solitude.

"Over there, Dad, look!"

Perched on a bale of straw, a rooster was on its way to the

sea.

"Too far off," the boatman observed. "We can't reach it now." And he turned the bow toward the floodplain.

On the embankment—a lost island in the ocean of flooding—lizards and snakes slithered; in the olive trees, birds chirped; and startled frogs leapt away and vanished into the grass. Beyond, in the devastated villages, other critters must have been in the same situation, sitting on the embankments' grass, waiting... Maybe they were gazing at the chapel of Our Lady of Alcamé—Lady of the Floods. But the tower's bell didn't ring... And the tugboat, the only one that passed through there, cost a hundred *mil-réis* an hour...

The boat with the white sail, the one which looked like a shroud, came gliding close along the embankment, loaded with people. As it crossed paths with the skiff, Manuel do Bote called out: "Safe journey!"

It was a sad journey. A boat weighed down with cargo, set to end up at some dock where there'd be no shelter. That's why the oarsman heard only the echo of his own voice. And Gineto remembered a certain ship—handkerchiefs waving from its rail, its white hull looking like a seagull's breast—to which he'd once wished a safe journey, too.

The afternoon was dying. On that sea of woe, shadows slid by, along with remnants of life left to save...

"Drop the grapple. I'm sick of water," Manuel do Bote said in a sorrowful voice.

He steered the bow toward land and moored.

III

THE WATER RECEDED from the fields, and the newspaper reports about the flood damages became scarce as well. The landowners' meeting had borne fruit—the embankments would be rebuilt. Meneses de Sá wouldn't sell his mansion in Estoril. And the fat gentleman, the one who smoked expensive cigars, was left waiting for another chance.

Only Coca was still complaining. "I'm screwed with this gig, man! More and more folks are out beggin'."

Sagui laughed. "Didn't I tell you?"

"If it was just weak kids like me... But grown men..."

"Tomorrow there'll be fewer," Malesso said. "Lots of folks are headin' to the fields."

He looked at his toe tracing patterns in the mud, then added, "I'm leavin' too. Just came to say goodbye to you all."

The others were stunned. "You said you'd never set foot there..."

"Yeah, well, my dad's earnin' nothin' at the dock, and we got seven mouths at home."

"Got the same at my place."

"Then why don't you come? With guys we know, it'd be better."

Guedelhas shook his head in refusal. And Gineto, silent until then, declared he wouldn't go even if they killed him. "Only in summer, and then just to catch birds."

"Easy for you to say when you got a sure thing. If my dad

owned a boat…"

"What good would that do? Ours is sittin' idle at the dock…"

"I still have hope…" Maquineta began.

But Sagui cut him off. "We know already—you're going to the Great Factory."

The others mocked him too, and Maquineta clammed up.

"How much are they paying you?" Gaitinhas asked Malesso.

"Four *mil-réis.*"

Madalena's son thought for a moment, then revealed what was troubling him, "If it were work I could handle, I'd go with you."

"Course you could, man!" Malesso exclaimed eagerly. "Haulin' dirt in carts—anyone knows how."

But Gineto cooled the enthusiasm. "Shut your trap! You gotta have muscle and stamina. By the end of the first day, this choir boy would be done for."

Gaitinhas looked back and forth between them, unable to decide.

"Come on, Gaitinhas. Four *mil-réis* is real money…"

"If my mom lets me… How long is it for?"

Malesso stuck out his lip. "About five weeks. But it's nearby. You can even see your house from there."

"Is it on Castro's embankments?" one of the boys asked.

Gaitinhas shuddered. He remembered Arturinho and the school, like a dream fading from memory. *Better to work for someone else.*

"If you want in," Malesso advised, "let me know today,

and I'll put in the request. We leave tomorrow."

The request... Gaitinhas thought. He'd also put in a request with Mr. Castro for the Great Factory—and the man hadn't even given him an answer.

He shook the hand of his departing friend, and the others, looking glum, did the same.

"Goodbye, Malesso. Good luck!" Gineto said, hugging his former rival.

"When this guy comes back, he'll talk our ears off with tall tales," Coca jeered.

But no one found it funny. Gaitinhas and Gineto struck up a quiet conversation. Maquineta had gone. And Sagui picked up his rickety handcart, which was loaded with clay he'd gathered from the hills.

"Forget about that," Guedelhas told him, scoffing at money hustles.

"No way—as long as there's dirty pots around, I'll get by."

And he started hollering down the street with his daily pitch, "Scouring powder! Two *tostões* a tin!"

GINETO had planned the raid for that week, when his father would be away with the boat. All he needed was to get two sacks and convince Gaitinhas, who refused to be a fruit thief.

That afternoon, however, his father called him down to the dock. A few boats had already left for other ports; the stevedores were swarming the gangplanks; and the *Boa Sorte*, moored side-on, was taking on cargo.

"We're heading out today," Manuel do Bote told him with a grin. "Got us a job to Montijo, paid right there at the dock."

Gineto stood silent, glancing sideways at the choppy river.

"You scared? A man like…"

"No, sir," his son cut in. "It's just that I had a little job lined up. You'd earn on your end… and I'd earn on mine."

"Oh… you're bailing on me, huh?!"

He scratched his three-day beard slowly, giving his thoughts some time, knowing he'd get nowhere by coming down hard.

"And here I was just sayin', loud enough for everyone to hear, that you'd go fearlessly even to Brazil."

"I would, Dad, but…"

Gineto rubbed his hands against his pants, as if trying to hold onto his crumbling resolve.

"But you're not going. You heard the floods sank some barges—so you're not going."

Malesso's father, who'd hoisted the last sack aboard, joined in: "You gonna leave your dad in the lurch, boy?! It's times like these that a skipper proves himself."

"He's scared," jeered Manuel do Bote, laying his hands on the boy's messy hair. "I was gonna give you that suit this time…"

Gineto shrugged, and Manuel do Bote took it as a sign of hesitation.

"God's truth!" he swore. "Even if I had to go hungry."

His son managed a smile. He was the one who'd been going hungry, ever since winter had set in…

"Well, Manel?" asked the Dock Warden, who'd since come

over. "You waiting for the boat to run aground?"

Manuel do Bote was about to answer, but his son blurted out first, "I'm comin', Dad—but not for the suit..."

They jumped onto the foredeck. "Hoist the foresail!" the skipper ordered, as he pulled the mooring lines in. Soaked with water, the sail slid along the stay like a battle flag; the skipper grabbed the tiller; and the fenders scraped along the edge of the dock in farewell.

Ti Bento came up right then, carrying bad omens. "Watch out, a storm's coming! Out by the bar, things are gettin' ugly..."

Manuel do Bote stretched out his arm to wave him goodbye and said some words that only the wind heard. Beneath the ribs of the boat, the river roared against the keel slicing through the high waters. It felt like the boat might split in two at any moment; but the big, bulging sail pushed it forward.

Gineto absorbed the sensations of that frightening voyage and smiled. Maybe his father thought he was there because of the lure of the new suit. *I'll explain the real reason—but only at the end of this trip, when I say goodbye to this boat forever,* he thought.

A seagull flew close by, battling the wind, and Manuel do Bote tracked it with his gaze until it vanished into the approaching mist. The pale light of the overcast sun was gradually fading away. With a steady hand on the tiller, indifferent to the icy spray of the waves, the skipper focused on the force of the elements. Black clouds charged in like steeds, and in the distance, the olive trees' branches begged the wind for mercy as it doubled its fury.

Ti Bento was right to warn us. We're in for a rough storm...

He turned the tiller, and the boat veered hard toward land.

"Lower the sails, Chico!"

But it was too late. A gust of wind tore the mainsail in a flash and hurled Gineto against the winch.

"Hold on!" yelled his father, hunching over the tiller.

A tall wave whipped the boat from bow to stern; another licked the tarps and penetrated the hull. Gineto slid jerkily until he reached the helmsman, who was now trying to retrieve the skiff.

"Dad, I'm not scared."

"Quick! Jump…"

"I'll go get the clothes."

He started back toward the bow, but the skipper held him back. "Jump… or we'll die here!"

Gineto got into the skiff, followed by his father. The waves rose as high as the pulleys; the boat had keeled over, and it was enveloped in water spray as thick as smoke. The sail's shreds had flown off like scared seagulls. And in the midst of the gale, standing tall like an indestructible marker, the bare mast pointed at the sky.

"Hold on to that oar!" shouted Manuel do Bote, as he slotted the other into the tholepin. But in the heart of the tempest, only gestures could speak. The skiff was at the mercy of the elements, at times rearing like a flying fish, at others hidden in the trough of the waves.

Between two big waves, the skipper saw the boat sink in an instant.

"Ah! You thief…" he sobbed. And he pulled at his hair in helplessness. The oar had slipped from his hands, and now, oblivious to the danger, he stared at the masthead sticking out of the water, as if he still hoped the *Boa Sorte* would resurface.

Gineto grabbed his arm and shook him, trying to give him courage. The wind seemed to be easing; but the skiff was filling with water. Behind one wave came another, and the sky grew darker still. For a brief moment, the boy tried to figure out whether he was crying, or if it was the water spray—sharp as needles—that was blurring his vision.

Suddenly, the skiff shattered against the shore with a dull thud. Amid the wreckage, an arm was groping for salvation. Gineto let out an anguished cry and plunged headlong into the waves. "Dad!" He dove once, twice, until he managed to grab hold of the inanimate body.

It all happened in a flash, between the flow and ebb of the same wave. Then came the struggle that seemed to last centuries: land just three metres from his hands—and those metres stretching into leagues. More effort—more exhaustion. His father's body slipping away from him—and his own will slipping too. A huge wave was cresting in front of him. It was death...

And then it was salvation. On the embankment, exhausted, father and son formed a single body. They lay there for a long time, until Gineto caught his breath, only to immediately lean over his father's deathlike face, a thin line of blood trickling down from it, staining his shirt red.

"Dad... my poor dad!" He began to cry. His body trembled from cold and despair. He remembered how once he'd been called a sissy for crying. But out here, he was just a child feeling lost and alone. He even felt scared! Now, free from the river, he feared the silence—the silence left behind after the roar of the waters and the half-closed eyes of his father.

Meanwhile, the wind was subsiding, and Gineto heard broken cries. He ran along the embankment that was narrowing between the waters and shouted for help too. Somewhere, in some cut-off thicket, there had to be people in danger. *If I could make out the terrain, I'd try to save them and myself. But what of my Dad...?* He turned back in distress, and found his father moaning his name and weeping like an infant. They gazed at each other, locking eyes, then hugged, silently sharing the joy of seeing each other again, as if each minute that had passed had been years of absence.

"Where are we?" Manuel do Bote asked.

"Dunno. A little while ago, I heard screams coming from that way..."

Their eyes scoured the fog, which was thick as night. It *was* night itself, for the sun had surely died in the storm.

"Look," his father pointed. "A light, over there..."

"They're car headlights."

It was a light that didn't guide sailors to a safe harbour. Manuel do Bote got up, staggering. "Let's shout. The wind's starting to shift direction. Maybe they'll hear us."

They shouted. Anguished voices answered them, nearby. Gineto thought he recognized one of them. "Malesso! You there, Malesso?"

"Yeah. Bring the boat over here, Gineto!"

Other people begged the two castaways to save them. They heard the high-pitched voices of women, the intermittent crying of a child...

"I can't!" Gineto yelled. "The skiff's gone."

He let himself slide down the embankment, probing the waters churning below.

"There's a deep spot here, Dad, and the current's pulling hard."

"It's a hollow left by the floods."

Now they knew where they were: on the Islet, near the mudflat the river had flooded. On the other side was Castro's embankment. And up on the roof of the hay barn were ditch-diggers and farmhands, the year-round workers and their families…

Caught off guard by the storm, they'd first taken shelter in the attic of the workers' lodge, without panic or disorder. It was the same every year… Two herders had even gone out to secure the cattle, fearing their boss might fire them for being careless. And out there they were, gone—stuck in the mud or swept away by the current.

One of the herders' wives started crying softly, but the farm overseer ordered her to hush.

"Don't worry, the devil looks after his own."

"You big baby…" Malesso's brother said, trying to cheer her up. "You're actin' like some city girl."

Little by little, however, the chatter turned to sobs. The waters kept rising, and the wind was growing fiercer.

A woman moaned, "It's the end of the world…" And just like that, panic swept through the old attic. Children were crying in the arms of their mothers, who were crouching in a corner. And Malesso, who'd never worked the fields, stared wide-eyed at the calm demeanor of some of the men and tried in vain to stop his teeth from chattering with fear.

An old man, stooped by the years and the toil, warned the overseer that the lodge was older than he was. "It'll come down any minute now…"

Moments later, the whole building shook. "Let's move to the hay barn!" the overseer ordered. "Women and children first."

Holding onto the men, with water up to their thighs, they managed to cross the courtyard. "Be brave! We'll be safe there."

With almost no strength left, they climbed up the bales of hay, their eyes wide as they watched the zinc roof break apart and fly off in pieces, and the floodwaters rising non-stop…

That's when the wind paused for a moment, and the two castaways shouted for help. Trembling, everyone looked toward the village, which must have been sound asleep, as not a single light had come on yet. And the sky held no promise of stars!

"Holy Lady of Alcamé…" prayed an old woman. But Our Lady of the Floods and the Fields was blocked off too.

"Keep your spirits up, folks!" the men encouraged. But they too were starting to falter. Another car's headlights—another hope that vanished. And so it went, no end in sight.

"What time could it be?" Manuel do Bote muttered.

His son didn't answer. Out there, time was measured in heartbeats.

Gineto was now thinking about his pals from the street and the tileries. He had roughed up some of them… He'd been a jerk, and yet he trusted they'd come for him. Afterward, Gaitinhas would play that song on his harmonica, the one

Gineto had heard him play up at Mirante; Sagui would tell a story about princes; and Pirica... *Why am I thinking of Pirica...? Oh, right... I stole the figs he meant for his grandmother on the day of 'God's bread'.* He'd let him join his gang. And the others too, because he was friends with them all, even Malesso, who was trembling just a stone's throw away. *Malesso! He never learned to swim with a proper stroke and always came last in the inlet races. He might die from fright alone, the poor guy!*

On a whim, he ran along the narrow ridge to go shout at the far end of the Islet, as if his buddies might hear his call from there. The wind answered him in the same tone, forcing him to turn back.

"If it shifts to a crosswind," Manuel do Bote predicted, "we're done for."

They could barely stand upright on the ridge now. "Lie down on this side, Chico."

They lay down on the embankment's slope, seeking shelter from the gale. The water started licking their feet, slowly, coldly; then, it bit into their legs.

"Hold onto the sedge, Dad."

Every now and then, the spray from the waves on their backs felt like dagger tips. More than the water, though, it was the night that froze their bodies.

"Tuck the little one inside your shirt," a young woman who was holding another infant reminded her husband. But the children's eyes were wide open to the night, and the cold pierced through their clothes. The barn's entire roof was gone. Clinging to the beams, the men held up their frail bodies.

Manuel do Bote and his son dug their nails into the

embankment's soil because the sedge had snapped. And the wind's stampede wouldn't stop!

The skipper grumbled, "Things would be better at the lodge; at least there's shelter there…"

Gineto could barely make out his father's words. Suddenly, a tremendous crash rose above the roar of the storm. The lodge had collapsed and smashed against the barn, splitting it in two, sweeping away people and beams alike.

Thuds… The death rattles of dying breaths… And one frenzied scream amid dozens of screams: "Toino! Toi… no."[33]

The gurgling of water like an insatiable throat. The neighing of horses in the distance. The beams whirling across the field until they slam into the southern embankment… And then the silence of mouths frozen in a grimace, and the grimace of mouths afraid to break the silence.

A strained voice: "Rosalina… where's our son?"

And another: "Felipe…"

Malesso clung to his brother's legs. "I'm here…"

Moans. Soft weeping from those who can no longer hear familiar voices… Not far off, the cries of someone being swept away by the current, maybe lying on a mat that once soothed exhaustion. But the waves, towering like moving mountains, impose the silence of death. Only an ox lows mournfully, then falls silent also.

Between each wave that engulfs him, Malesso keeps seeing the terrified eyes of two heads caught between the beams. He wants to ask them to close their eyelids—but he can't. He wonders if they're still alive and shuts his own eyes. But then the faces come closer, and they're skulls, like the ones he once saw at the cemetery years ago. His arms weaken; his whole body trembles. He can no longer clench his teeth, which chatter from cold and fear—mostly from the cold, as the water's up to his chest. He lifts his head toward his brother; he opens his mouth in a plea, but a wave muffles him... His hands slowly slip away.

Upright, hanging from a beam, Malesso's brother sees nothing, nor does he feel any weight lifting from his frozen legs. The storm is beginning to tire. The flood eases.

"Look," someone says. "Seems like a light's coming over there..."

"It is!"

"Let's all shout together."

They raise their voices, and other voices reach them.

"Louder!"

"I can't. My throat's gone..."

"Louder!"

The light zigzagged through the darkness, and once again the distant clamour drew closer to the survivors. On the other embankment, Gineto started shouting as loud as he could, too. His fingernails were bloody and half his body was submerged. Even so, what made him shudder more was the slimy touch of snakes and crickets that brushed against his face.

"It's no use calling," his father remarked after a while. "We can hear them, but they can't hear us because the wind's cutting across now."

"But it's eased up, Dad."

"It's no use."

The light gradually faded away... The night grew darker

with uncertainty. And Gineto broke into sobs.

✦ ✦ ✦

AT THE DOCK, with hands clasped and eyes trying to pierce the thick fog, men and women wait in torment. Some have their homes flooded, their furniture broken apart; but they stay there, feet in the water, helpless.

"What about the tugboat?"

"I hear one went to the fields already."

"No way. The car hasn't had time to reach Lisbon yet…"

They fall silent, willing the car forward in their minds.

Maria do Bote weeps softly, and her children, clinging to her skirt, join the chorus. The Dock Warden reappears.

"Well then, Master Antoino?"[34]

"Don't bother me! I've already taken measures."

And he goes back to the tavern. But they pester him there too.

"Master Toino…"

All eyes fix on the man's aged forehead as he downs his glass and stares at its bottom, not saying a word. He's thinking he'd never seen such a storm, not in decades. It had always been easy for him to settle disputes and maintain order at the dock. But now… He turns to the mariners. "What am I supposed to do? Tell me…" And he crosses his trembling arms.

"Master Toino, please requisition the tugboat…"

"I already did!"

"We'll all go. We can take a launch and skiffs."

The mariners explain what they'd do, if only they could. And the Dock Warden jams his cap down on his head and hurries off. He knows the tugboat will come only after the storm dies down, when it's no longer needed in Lisbon. Nevertheless, he knocks on the gate at the High Farm. Then he climbs the staircase, which the waters haven't flooded.

"Mr. Castro, those people…"

"Listen, let's not mistake the cloud for Juno!"[35]

The mariner crumples his cap in his hands, not understanding.

"Obviously it's not pleasant to spend a night out in the open. But the barns are tall, damn it…"

His mood now soured, he sits down in an armchair, checks the time, and yawns. He'd spent the whole day tied up at the conference—serious work, in which he was set to refute all prior reports on the nature of the floods. He'd gone to bed worried about the damages at the embankment. And now they'd come to wake him up at midnight!

"It's a sea of tears down at the dock, Mr. Castro."

"Sentimental nonsense."

"They're blaming me…"

The man stops mid-sentence, not daring to reveal what people are saying about the landowner. But the latter guesses the rest.

"Aren't you the authority? Assert yourself. Ultimately, this is dangerous agitation that must be stamped out at once. If necessary, call in the police."

"I requisitioned a tugboat, Mr. Castro, but it's taking time…" He twists his cap further and adds, "You could hire one, sir..."

"Me? Not a chance!"

Nevertheless, he reconsiders. *A few dozen head of cattle might be worth the tugboat's steep fee. But at this hour...*

He stands up, puts his meaty hand on the Dock Warden's shoulder, and says, "Of course I care about those people's fate. But it's late; the dead can't be saved now. Care for a glass of Port, master?"

"Thank you, but no."

"Well, tell them down at the dock that I'm going to take action. You can count on me."

The Dock Warden returns to the dock, and Mr. Castro tiptoes back to bed so as not to wake Arturinho.

Meanwhile, Malesso's father and another mariner set out into the storm in a flatboat lit by a kerosene lamp. From the dock, weeping eyes of widows follow them.

"It's madness," says Ti Bento.

The Dock Warden protests when he finds out. "On top of everything else! Then they'll say it was my fault. Bunch of roughnecks!"

Shadows move about; the night intensifies rumours and speculation. And the lamp's light zigzags through the fog, as uncertain as the fate of men.

Skippers and crewmen watch over the boats and reinforce the ropes. Another man is salvaging logs and wailing, "Ah! Thief... You thief!" It's all he can say. Of the colourful launch— the one with the name *Benvinda* between painted flowers on its bow—only half of its mast is visible at the edge of the dock.

"Leave the logs, man," someone tells him. "Let your boss

come get them."

But he stays hunched over, weeping. "Ah! Thief... You thief of a sea!"

The boys from the tileries aren't sleeping either. At that hour, Arturinho is dreaming of toys, while they're restlessly pacing back and forth.

"You stayin' here all night, Sagui?" one asks.

"What else? The hayloft caved in..."

"Now what?

"I'll go back to sleeping under doorways."

"Same here. Even if I wanted to," Guedelhas says, "I couldn't go lie down. My bed's soaking wet."

Gaitinhas thinks of those fighting the floods and remarks, "Gineto's got it worse."

"At least he knows how to swim, but Malesso..."

"What good's knowing how to swim, man?"

Sagui insists it matters. "That guy can cross the river from bank to bank..."

"In the summer, even I can."

"You? Get real, kid!"

Most of them assert that Gineto can beat the fury of the waves. Then, Gaitinhas suggests they all go out on the launch when the tugboat arrives. The group perks up. Only Coca, who's crippled, pleads in a quavering voice for them to bring back his older brother. But the hours pass, and Malesso's father returns disheartened.

"If only we had some light..." someone remarks.

Sagui's stars had forgotten to light the lamps at the street corners.

✦ ✦ ✦

DAWN was breaking when the tugboat set out along with Zé Pirica's launch and two skiffs. The storm had passed; the tide was ebbing.

Far from the dock now, Gaitinhas and his pals emerged one by one from the stern cabin, to the crew's astonishment.

"What's this now? Who gave you lot permission to board the boat?"

Gaitinhas stepped forward. "Sorry, we didn't mean to cause trouble."

"We got family out in the fields," Sagui added.

"I don't want the responsibility. Damn kids! You're going back to the dock in a skiff, and quick."

"Mr. Zé…"

"I've told you!"

That's when Pirica begged his uncle to let them stay. "We'll help out, uncle."

"It's dangerous, you know?"

"We're not scared."

The skipper smiled, and so did Gaitinhas, despite the fear he felt. It was his first time on the river, whose muddy waters, whipped by the wind, roared against the boat like wild beasts.

From time to time, a wave lashed the boys' faces, but they stayed alert, watching the fog dissipate, though the dawn still carried the night's uncertainty.

"Look, over there," Maquineta pointed feverishly. "It's

people…"

"You blind, boy? Those are fallen trees," the skipper explained.

But Gaitinhas quickly whispered, "Hear that…?"

"What? It's the wind."

"Sounds like moaning. Who knows—maybe Gineto's seen us already…"

The others strained their ears. On land, the hills themselves leaned forward in silent questioning over the floodplain, which was dull and yellowish like the skin of a dying old woman.

"Uncle, can we go up to the bow?"

"No. You're fine where you are."

"If he'd let us… I'd even climb the mast."

They kept staring at the mist, at the tugboat's dark silhouette, at the boundless river. And they imagined themselves as lookouts on a ship bound for strange lands, amid dangers and reefs.

Suddenly, the tugboat's low-pitched whistle roused everything. And as if by magic, the broken-down barns of the Islet emerged from the waters, in the distance. Gaitinhas rubbed his astonished eyes; his friends peered into the mist. And again the whistle's sound rolled mournfully from embankment to embankment. A seagull flapped its wings against the wind. The silence deepened.

"They're all dead," Guedelhas murmured.

His friends trembled with anguish, and Zé Pirica, who'd signaled to stop, began letting out the towline as the launch approached land. In their impatience, the boys grabbed onto the slimy beams of the old dock above. But once they reached the top of the embankment slope, they wanted to turn back. Gaitinhas started crying.

"Is this what you came here for?" the skipper scolded, but he too stopped in dismay. Atop what was left of a roof and piles of debris lay curled-up, half-naked bodies; others had their lifeless faces turned skyward and seemed to be sleeping. Farther away were oxen and horses with bloated bellies, and crownless tree trunks looking as sad as cypresses. Mats floated on the water. And standing on a dry strip of land, a brown horse was perhaps trying to recognize the meadow where it had once grazed.

"Pull up the skiff!" Zé Pirica ordered, his voice unsteady. "Quickly…"

The boys grabbed hold of the boat, bending their backs as their legs sank into the mud, and the mariners urged them on.

"Now's the time to show you're men. Put your backs into it!"

The skiff moved grudgingly; anxiety gripped their chests.

"If I could just plant my feet…" lamented Guedelhas, who fancied himself an athlete.

"One more heave. We're almost there…"

They finally reached the top, panting and sweating despite the icy downpour that had begun falling.

"Now we'd better rig up a rope ferry," said the skipper, who'd gone back to fetch some heavy ropes. "Anyone who can't swim stays here."

Gaitinhas sat on the ground next to Maquineta, ignoring the rain, his eyes fixed on the rope that slithered like a water snake. He began counting the oar strokes, then the bodies being carried onto the skiff. *Is Malesso one of them? And where's Gineto?*

The distant voices of his friends didn't answer his questions, nor Maquineta's, who trembled with impatience as he thought of a faster and safer ferry system. But the skiff returned.

"Survivors, Mr. Zé?"

The skipper wiped his eyes with the back of his hand and answered, "We have more of the dead than the living."

They began unloading the bodies. Gaitinhas shuddered as he felt the icy touch of their hands. Maquineta noticed the skinny, purplish thighs of two little girls, but immediately averted his gaze, wishing he hadn't looked. From shaking so much, one woman seemed to still be rocking the cold child she was holding in her arms. Malesso's brother rolled his eyes in their haunted sockets, seeking the light the waters had stolen from him.

"Where's your brother?" Gaitinhas asked him in a low voice. He tensed his face for a moment and remained silent, oblivious to everything.

Then, while the launch ferried those people to the tugboat, another launch came, and then another. Exhausted, the boys let a body slip down the embankment, and Zé Pirica got angry.

"He's dead…" Gaitinhas said by way of excuse. But he broke into tears, as if he'd desecrated the body.

Finally, the tugboat departed, and the men from the launch and the boys skirted the island in search of more people.

Daylight was breaking. The lodge's ruins could now be made out more clearly: only a corner of the walls remained, along with the chimney, still intact though useless now. All around lay farming equipment, bales of hay, and the black shape of a flatboat that the flood had dragged there.

The skipper entered the cabin, bringing out bread and two pieces of sausage, which he handed out to the boys. "I take it you haven't lost your appetite…"

"I wasn't even thinkin' of that," Sagui answered.

The others tried to shake off the sadness. "You gobbler! You'd eat a whole ox…"

"We'll go get one right now," Zé Pirica joked.

But the sight of the corpses dried up both laughter and hunger. Gaitinhas felt sick. And Sagui remembered the horse that had survived the storm.

"Mr. Zé, we could go save the horse… The one that was left stranded out there."

"You're crazy. Let the owner go get it."

"It doesn't have an owner now. It belongs to whoever saves it."

"Sure it does… You'd be stealin' the horse, and Castro would throw you in jail."

The boys hesitated. "I only wanted to…" Sagui began, still insisting.

But he left the sentence hanging, because Gaitinhas let out a cry and pointed to the embankment, where two bodies lay stretched out.

"That's Gineto!"

In a flash, they jumped into the skiff and landed with water up to their waists. But Gaitinhas—pale, biting his fingers— didn't even have the heart to leave the launch.

They turned over the castaways, who were lying face down

with their hands buried in mud up to their wrists. Gineto groaned; his father opened his eyes.

"They're still alive, boys!"

And it was as if, amid cypresses, two bodies had come back to life.

The anguish came back later at the lodge, as they recovered more of the dead, and it was even greater at the dock, when they returned.

A high tide of tears and screams... The anxious eyes of those still hoping... The words that counted for nothing...

Malesso's father moves from boy to boy, grabbing their arms. "Where's my son Felipe? Why didn't you bring back my boy?"

Maria do Bote cries on and on, no longer even knowing why. Off in a corner of the dock, Ti Bento mumbles curses and rasps, "Now go ahead, blame the sea. Fools..."

IV

LOOKING PALE and still carrying the shadow of tragedy in his eyes, but ready to face more—as the doctor had put it—Gineto left the hospital.

The friendly nurse patted him on the back. "Goodbye, walking dead," he said, laughing.

"Thanks for everything, Mr. Nurse, sir…"

But he saved his hugs of gratitude for his buddies—he'd never forget them.

"If you guys hadn't come for me…"

"You were the brave one. It even made the newspaper."

"They say you saved your dad twice…"

Gineto smiled with no trace of vanity. His friends crowded around him like he was a hero, asking him to tell the story of his feat. He refused.

"I'll tell you later."

Sagui remembered the argument from the night of the storm and jabbed at Gaitinhas. "Didn't I tell you he'd make it?"

The other boy said nothing. Gineto was looking at them all like he was seeing them for the first time. These weren't the boys he'd fought and bickered with so often. Or maybe he was the one who'd changed, as even the street seemed different to him, less grim.

"I got something for you guys," he said. He pulled his hand from his pocket and offered them cigarettes.

"Whoa! These are the fancy ones…" Guedelhas exclaimed. "You rich now, pal?"

"Some ladies came by the hospital and handed out money."

The pack made its way from hand to hand. Gineto tucked the rest of the cigarettes away, saying they were for Malesso. His friends glanced at each other, and one of them said, "So you don't know?"

"Know what?"

"Malesso died out there in the fields."

Gineto opened his mouth, but the words dried up in his throat. It was Guedelhas who broke the silence, commenting, "He wanted to own a farm… and never even made it to overseer."

"That's fate," murmured Gaitinhas, thinking how he'd wanted to go work in the fields too.

"His dad's going crazy looking for him. And his brother might go blind from all the water that hit his eyes."

Sagui jumped in to share what he'd heard. "They say a light appears every night where Malesso died. Could be his ghost…"

The group shuddered, but Gineto called it a sick fiction, the kind Sagui was always spinning. But Sagui insisted, "On my life, that's what I heard down at the dock. They said they even took a launch out there, but the light vanished."

They went quiet, then a spooked Gaitinhas asked, "Have you ever seen a ghost, Sagui?"

"Sure have. Once, when I was with a circus…"

And his friends listened in silence as Sagui recounted his vagabond adventure. Then the rain pulled the boys' attention away, and one of them sighed. "I wish summer was here already."

"You missin' the tileries, eh?"

"Nah, but at least you make some money. And there's fruit to fill your belly."

Guedelhas brought up the job he'd been promised once the soccer championship finished. "I'm gonna play on trial," he said. "If they like me, they'll get me work."

"You don't have the build to play," Pirica shot back with envy. "One hard hit and you'll go flying."

"No worries. As long as they give me the job."

"Maquineta's already got one at the Great Factory," Sagui joked. "He's workin' as a maid."

The gang laughed at the reference to the food basket Maquineta now took to his uncle every day, aiming to gawk at the machines. Long before noon, he'd already be pestering the gatekeeper: "Please let me in…"

"Wait for the whistle."

"Come on… My mom told me not to be late…"

He'd cross the gate and forget all about his mother and the lunch, as he'd get dizzy with excitement over the lathes, shafts, and gears in motion. When his uncle worked the night shift, Maquineta would get ecstatic with all the lights and the engines sounding louder. Later, as he lay on his damp straw bed, he'd fall asleep happily turning it all over in his mind.

His friends, however, wouldn't let up with the teasing.

"What he carries in that basket is his metalworker's tools."

Maquineta fired back with curses and dirty gestures. "The tool's right here. Wanna see it?"

But Gineto put an end to the argument by revealing his plan to steal oranges, which everyone jumped at the chance to join. Only Gaitinhas was still just as hesitant as when he was first invited.

"What about you, Gaitinhas?"

He thought for a moment about his sick mother and the job that was taking forever to come through.

"Maybe I'll go, but…"

"You scared? Chicken!"

His face went red. "No, but I'd be ashamed of being a thief."

"It's only fruit…"

"It's still stealing," he argued. "Those oranges have an owner. And if he catches us…"

Gineto doubled down. "The owner's Castro and others like him, who are a bunch of misers. Did that guy give anything to Coca, who lost his brother and is out beggin' now?"

Gaitinhas still hesitated. He thought of Arturinho's disdain, of Mr. Castro's empty promise, of the angry words at the dock when they brought in the dead. And he wavered.

"Maybe we'll find work…"

"Yeah, at the tilery, come summer," Guedelhas scoffed.

Gineto pressed on. "So you feel sorry for those guys, but not your own mom. You're a little shit."

"Fine, I'll go," Gaitinhas said quietly. And whether for his mother's sake or his own, his eyes welled up with tears.

✦ ✦ ✦

IT WAS a moonless night, drizzly and cold—fit only for vagabonds, like the wind. That's why Gineto chose it. Cunningly, with no rush, he had spent a week scoping out the valley and tracking the moon. His impatient friends kept coming up to him. "Well? You waitin' for the oranges to run out?"

He'd answer like a leader: "I got this. Just wait."

And that night, as soon as the sun died out, he gave the word: "Midnight, at Mirante."

Gaitinhas left the door unlocked, dropped his clothes at the foot of the bed, and lay down. His heart was pounding so hard he feared his mother might hear it in the silence of the hovel. He stayed alert to her breathing and to the chimes from the church tower. He counted eleven strikes. His mother coughed deeply. *Could it be midnight?* he wondered. He'd been waiting so long… He decided to put on his pants under the bedcovers. *What if my mom sees me open the door?* He hesitated. He'd counted to eleven… But the fear of showing up late and being branded a coward got him to his feet. He was halfway across the house when his mother spoke.

"Are you getting up, João?"

"Just stepping outside…"

"Make sure you bundle up…"

"Sure, Mom."

He buttoned his shirt tighter and stepped out into the cold night. From the village came the sound of voices and music chords—some tavern was still open. As he climbed the hillside, Gaitinhas regretted leaving so early, because Mirante was deserted and the sky was starless. Upon reaching the top, he peered into the shadows. No one. It really was only eleven. Just then, he heard a voice ask, "Who's there?"

He shivered. It sounded like Sagui's voice... The boy hopped over the parapet and came to meet him.

"Scared you, pal?"

"You got here early," Gaitinhas said.

"Being here or down below, same difference."

"Where are you sleeping now?"

"In the old chapel. I'm a little saint..." He laughed, and Gaitinhas found himself admiring his friend, who was smaller, maybe even younger, yet unafraid of the night and one who smiled at misfortune. Then they both turned their gaze toward the dark blot of the floodplain and the river, dotted with flickering lights, that stretched out without end.

"Could one of those be Malesso's light?"

"No, those are fishing lights," Sagui explained. "Malesso's light shows up at dawn, at the hour he died."

Despite his fear, Gaitinhas listened attentively to more stories about ghosts and goblins. Meanwhile, the midnight chimes rang from the tower, sounding like a death knell. And the shadowy figures of his friends, as they arrived, seemed like Sagui's ghosts to him.

Gineto, holding two sacks, organized the gang. One of the boys asked, "Where are we going?"

"To the High Farm."

"The caretaker's got a rifle, Gineto..."

"Let him. We're gonna steal all of Castro's oranges." He pointed to Maquineta. "You and Gaitinhas will stand guard by the road and the gate. One at each spot..."

"I'd rather go inside," Maquineta protested.

Faced with the prospect of being left alone, Gaitinhas would've also preferred to take his chances in the orchard. But the leader kept his orders, declaring, "You guys don't have experience yet."

They set off. The darkness slid down from the hills, transforming the valley into a forest of shadows. The wind drew hums from the clay pots on windmill sails[36]. And the dampness clung to their bodies like birdlime.

Afraid of falling behind, Gaitinhas quickened his pace. He tried to strike up conversation with his friends, but Gineto imposed silence. *If only I could whistle away my fear...*

At a certain point, they stopped. Gineto handed one of the sacks to Sagui. "Hide it in the vineyard," he whispered. "If you hear the signal, you know what to do..." The boy vanished into the darkness, with Pirica behind him, while Gineto tossed the other sack over the wall.

"Let's jump over at the corner. There aren't any glass shards on top there," he said.

"It's dangerous. The caretaker sets traps there."

Gineto climbed onto his buddy's shoulders and then hoisted himself up with his hands.

If the glass cuts the sack... Gaitinhas thought. But his friend vanished behind the wall. Guedelhas signaled for his help, too. Gaitinhas bent his back, and his legs wobbled under the other boy's weight.

"I can't..." he groaned, overwhelmed with shame.

"You have to!"

He braced himself against the wall and gritted his teeth. A deep pain dug into his lower back. He was trembling, but held on as long as needed. Then he was left alone, peering into the darkness with bulging eyes. Fear clung to his skin like the damp to his clothes. Only now did he notice those sad, monotonous moans drifting down from the hill. *Is it the wind?* he wondered. He remembered the ghosts that spooked Sagui when he had roamed the land.

Slowly, he directed his thoughts to pleasant things. He pictured himself again at the end of his first school exam, when Mr. Mesquita had told the proctor, "This boy's going places…" But a dog howled, and other dogs joined in. The intermittent croaking of a frog lent bad omens to the night. Gaitinhas's thoughts fled away from school and latched onto the trees shadowing the road—trees split at the crown, becoming corpses in the flooded plain… *Oh, if only I could at least whistle the fear away…*

But whistling was the danger signal for his buddies, who were counting on him to keep watch. They too were trembling in the shadows. Even Gineto was crawling through the garden, holding his breath, uneasy—as if this raid were different from all the others. *Stealing oranges to eat or sell… It's all the same,* he thought. The only differences were the night, with its sparse stars, and the sodden ground that clung to him, bogging down his movements. *Sagui must be crouching amid the vines, invisible. But I have to crawl like a toad…* His shirt had bunched up to his chest, and he felt his pants slipping at the hips, despite the rope holding them up. How he longed for summer, when the wet grass brushed bare skin! Crickets would sing; the scent of flowers would fill his nose and pores; the warm earth felt like a woman's embrace… It was worth crawling like a toad in the summer. He wouldn't give a damn about the dogs and caretakers then, and he'd surrender his body over to that slow pleasure that danger only made more intense.

With his belly exposed and his hands covered in mud, Guedelhas was cursing his luck also. "Not even a hot girl could warm me up now…" he griped.

Gineto clapped a dirty hand over his mouth and pointed to a figure that, just steps away from the orchard, was blocking their path. They stopped, trembling. The figure wasn't moving, but it was definitely a man—hat tilted, legs apart, standing firm like someone waiting… Guedelhas thought he could even make out the man's harsh features and bristly beard.

"What do we do?" they asked, eyeing each other. "Turn back? What about the others?" Gineto thought he couldn't leave them to fend for themselves like before, because in this gang, risks and profits were shared equally. More than the duty of gratitude toward those who'd saved his life, his duty as a leader demanded that he not run away. Now he understood why this raid was unlike all the others.

The figure remained still and silent, barring the path to the orchard. The boys were starting to despair when a break in the clouds brightened the night for a moment. Gineto smiled, and his buddy let out a deep breath. It was just a scarecrow in a sown garden patch.

"Quick… Sagui and Pirica probably have their sack half full by now."

They slipped into the orchard, which was as silent as an

abandoned cloister.

"Don't pick them all from the same tree…" Gineto warned as he stuffed oranges into the makeshift pouch of his shirt. Every so often, he'd dump them into the sack and patrol the orchard. All that could be heard was the rustle of branches bending under Guedelhas's nervous hands.

"The sack's nearly full… Hurry up."

Gineto, however, would've liked to stay there all night savouring the danger even more than the oranges they'd have later.

From the direction of the mansion, a guard dog barked, sniffing out the boys, and shadows came swirling through the grove. Fear led to snapped twigs.

"Run! The big dog's coming!" Guedelhas shouted as he darted through the trees.

"Give me a hand, man!"

They both grabbed the sack, which dragged along the ground, knocking over vines. The barking drew closer.

Out on the road, Gaitinhas measured his friends' panic against his own, from when he played in Arturinho's garden and the German shepherd came creeping up, growling with suspicion at his worn-out clothes…

Guedelhas felt his strength failing. "Let's ditch the sack, Gineto!"

"No!"

The vines scraping against his legs felt like canine teeth. He tripped over one and went sprawling into a puddle in the garden. The frog went quiet, but the night's bad omens lingered. Dragged down in the fall, Gineto choked back furious curses.

At the other end of the orchard, there was a commotion of voices and dogs being egged on, "Get 'em, Rex..."

Right afterward, a gunshot shook the whole valley. A rooster mistook the hour and crowed. And the gunshot's echo, bouncing from hill to hill, sounded to Gaitinhas like a volley of rifles. In terror, his mind fled back to the flooded fields where corpses floated, their pale faces taking on the features of his friends. Far off, the windmill sails played the wind's grim symphony, interspersed with barking and other noises...

Gaitinhas began to cry softly, like a lost child. Just then, Pirica and Sagui reached the road.

"Take this, Gaitinhas. I can't carry it anymore," Pirica pleaded.

The boy slung the sack over his shoulder and followed them in silence, his head down to hide his tears.

Shortly after, Guedelhas and Maquineta appeared too, gasping for air, and the others all asked at once, "What about Gineto? Where is he?"

"He went back for the sack we left in the vineyard."

"What if they catch him?"

"I sure warned him. But he said we needed those oranges..."

They sat down to wait for their leader, and Sagui told them about his escape like it was some tall tale. "...the big dog was almost on top of me. I tossed him a bread crust. He let out a growl, bit into it, and I jumped over the wall."

"You're lyin', Sagui."

"It's true, buddy. Ask Pirica."

Pirica smiled cheerfully, and Gaitinhas remarked, "He doesn't like bread. What he eats is the meat Arturinho gives him."

"No way!"

Sagui cut the story short in envy of a purebred dog that turned up its nose at bread crusts and had never had to rummage for leftover food in garbage bins.

SPRING

I

WISPS OF CLOUDS in the sky, like the flock of white doves that used to brush past Mirante. A cloud of blossoms in the valley's trees. The sky lending its blue to the calm river, with no remorse for the floods that hardly anyone remembers anymore.

Coca still begs at doorsteps. "Spare a little something... My brother died in the floods..." But one of these days, he'll end up joining Gineto's gang.

Some men wear tight black suits and walk the streets as if it were Sunday, but it won't be long before they return to the fields. Castro's already talked about rebuilding the breached embankments and rebuilding the workers' lodge.

"Are you going?" one of them asks.

"What choice do I have? We're just walkin' around here with nothin' to do..."

"When I remember that..."

He cuts the sentence short so as not to remember. The tree branches that the storm snapped are trying to revive. And so are the men. Only Malesso's brother will forever carry that winter night of anguish in his eyes... And the woman whose baby died hasn't lost the rocking motion in her arms.

They call her mad for it.

✦ ✦ ✦

MANUEL do Bote sawed the planks salvaged from the river and set about patching up holes in his house of wood and tin that the gale had torn apart.

These days, he was rising with the stars, before the clock went off, as if his boat were loaded with cargo and waiting for him.

"Why are you getting up so early, Manel?"

"I'm sick of bed."

His wife would say nothing so as not to upset him, and he'd head down to the dock, through the mist that blurred the names and colours of the moored boats, giving him the illusion that the *Boa Sorte* had returned overnight to nestle by the seawall. Later, when the sun revealed their outlines, he'd trudge back home.

His wife and Deolinda would be at the factory; his little children would be crawling in the inlet; and he'd spend the whole day alone, doing carpentry work and daydreaming that the house was his boat, under repair at the shipyard.

When the work was done, he even built a toy for little Tonecas[37] and brought it to him at the inlet.

"Here's a boat for you."

Startled, staring at the hairy hands of the man who'd only ever given him slaps, his son didn't move.

"It's for you, you dummy."

Wary, he grabbed the boat with a trembling hand. His sister stopped kneading mud and pouted.

"Want too…"

"No! It's mine…"

Manuel do Bote had to step in to stop the children's squabble. He sat with them by the water's edge, and the three of them made waves so the boat could sail.

Eventually, his hands fell still. His spirits moved like the river tide—now rising with hopeful plans, now ebbing into hopelessness.

"Listen, man!" said Zé Pirica. "That's no way to live. Wanna come work on my boat?"

He shook his head no. *I'd rather dig from sunup to sundown with my own hoe in the valley's estates.*

That's what he thought, yet he wouldn't leave the dock. He wandered there in zigzags, lending a hand with planks and moorings, or chewing on hopes.

"If you hear of a boat needing a skipper, over on the other bank…"

"Don't worry," his friend would reply. One barge would arrive, another would set off.

"See about that for me, Zé…"

"I won't forget. Soon as I hear something…"

Ti Bento told him off upon hearing his gripes and gloom. "You're all actin' like slugs now. When you fall into the sea, you grab onto whatever you can find."

Manuel do Bote cast his eyes across the dock without answering the old man's rant.

"When you fall into the sea..." He'd said as much when he'd worked the tileries, the embankments, and the vineyard furrows. But in the end, he lost everything in a single night, along with his faith in work.

Still, at suppertime, the soup tasted as bitter as medicine. *Living off my wife's soup...* he thought.

The children scraped their plates clean and asked for just a little more.

"There's no sating them, damn it!" their mother grumbled.

Tonecas hurled his plate and muttered every swearword he'd picked up; his sister burst into a wail.

"Grab that child, Deolinda! You all treat me like a pack mule, but one day I'll snap."

Gineto eyed his mother's pregnant belly and smiled. Manuel do Bote took his wife's nagging upon himself and lowered his head over his plate. *Bitter soup, that one...*

The next day, he begged for the position left vacant by Malesso's father, who had quit the dock, and took up work as a cargo hauler by land and sea. It was a new path, one that demanded a strong arm and a chest of steel.

That evening, with a work bag hanging from his arms, he walked into the Skippers' Tavern, right by the river, to listen to the melodic cadence of the surf and Chico Lindinho's *fados*.

"Care for a drink, Manel?"

"No, thanks. I had two and a half glasses with supper, and that's enough."

"Come on, I'm payin'."

His mouth was dry and his breathing tight. He accepted the drink. Chico Lindinho, with a syrupy voice, sang a few verses in praise of wine. The tavern keeper grinned and poured another round. Shortly after, more patrons burst in, arm in arm with the Madwoman, who was dishevelled and drunk.

"Get us some wine! This gal's gonna sing *fado*, Lindinho."

She filled the place with screams. Pale and gaunt, her body swaying in her clothes of mourning, she drooled wine and insults.

Zé Pirica rested his sad eyes on her and said, "This life ain't worth a damn. Shall we call it a night, Manel?"

They left, and the cool night air eased Manuel do Bote's wine-soaked dizziness.

Still, at the door to his house, he picked a fight with Deolinda for being with her boyfriend at that hour. His wife told him to hush so as not to wake their little children. He barked back, "*You* hush, I say! Who's in charge here, huh? Who?"

That night was the prelude to shouting and tears, which only Gineto could put an end to. The boy would step in and hold back his stumbling father, who would then whimper in a tearful voice, "You too? You saved my life and now you turn on me..."

"Go to bed, Dad."

"The *Boa Sorte* is loaded at the dock... That's where I wanna sleep..."

Gineto remembered the struggle against the waves. He recalled his father braced at the helm, chest to the swells—and now here he was, falling down drunk. He felt sorry for him. He'd help him to bed, like he'd done on the Islet's track on the night of the storm. Afterward, he'd go join his friends at

Mirante.

Spring was breathing energy and hope into everything, and with the orange business booming, all the boys were in good spirits. Madalena seemed to rejuvenate, like the dwarf pear tree in the garden of the old house where she once had lived, and Gaitinhas no longer cast wistful looks over the floodplain, longing for his father and school. He now turned toward the valley, which resembled Mr. Castro's garden. Lush wheat fields rippled across the hillside; the almond trees were clouds fallen from the deep-blue sky; and on the winding ridge of the hills, off in the distance, the windmills—like hand-cranked music boxes—played a melody just like the one Gaitinhas had heard one afternoon at Arturinho's house.

When there wasn't a raid planned, the boys would gather in the ruins of the chapel where Sagui lived.

"Step right in, gentlemen, step right in!" he'd joke, adopting mannerisms he'd learned at the circus.

"Where's last night's loot?"

"Loot? Only respectable people live here, Mr. Gineto."

And he'd laugh as he led his friends through the maze of stones and debris.

Gaitinhas was the one in charge of counting the oranges, since—according to Sagui—he knew all the numbers up to a thousand, which amazed everyone.

Suspicious and envious, Pirica once tried to dethrone him. "I'll count," he said one day.

"Mind you, there's over a hundred oranges here…"

"I can count to zillions if I want."

But when he got to thirty-nine, he had to give up. From

then on, Gaitinhas rose in rank within the gang: he divided up the money, kept track of the leftover fruit, and once even wrote a letter for Guedelhas to send to his girlfriend.

"What do you want me to say?" he'd asked, more flustered than on exam day.

"Dunno... That I'm smitten with her... And that she should come watch me play on Sunday."

"But does she know how to read, Guedelhas?"

"No. But that's okay."

He spent an entire afternoon and two sheets of paper on it; but he ended it with a kiss, written in clear handwriting with a pen nibbled at the tip.

✦ ✦ ✦

ONE NIGHT, Sagui woke up with a start to the sound of someone grumbling. He curled up tighter against the stones and pulled the patchwork blanket over his head. But the voice pierced the covers, just as clearly as he could hear the thumping of his heart in his chest. *Who can it be at this hour? Perhaps a thief who has found the fruit stash, or a spy sent by Mr. Castro...*

High-pitched and raspy, the voice sounded like a woman's. *Maybe it's one of the guys in disguise, playing a prank...* He peeked through a tear in the blanket. In the dim moonlight, he could make out a dark figure sprawled on a pile of rubble, as if lying in wait also. Sagui longed for the vineyard hut where he used to sleep, where nothing ever reached him but the barking of dogs.

What if that's a rabid dog? A shiver froze his body and the stone bed. *No. It's a woman's voice.* Now he could hear muffled moans and jumbled words… Then, silence pressed down on his eyelids. He shut his eyes, his attention drifting, but soon opened them again to watch the motionless figure. Eventually, exhaustion made him fall into a deep sleep.

When he woke up, the day was still slumbering, and so was the figure. He approached it.

It was the Madwoman. His first instinct was to flee before she launched into one of her fits that would send her chasing after street kids with stones and screams. But then he saw her pale face smeared with blood. He remembered the woman who'd come on the launch—the one crying and rocking her dead child—and took pity.

Gently, he dabbed at her wound with a wet rag. She opened her dazed eyes to him, held him in her arms, called him her little boy. Sagui wanted to break free from those cold hands caressing him, but out of fear, he let himself be rocked like an infant as he watched the Madwoman sideways. Through the neckline of her blouse, he could see a stark white breast and a dark bruise on her neck.

"You've grown so much, my little boy…"

Her smile was a grimace of sorrow. Sagui attempted a caress that dissipated in the air, then turned his face further away. Yet his eyes remained hypnotized by the glimpse of her breast. Against his will, his trembling, pleading hand reached for the neckline too… The Madwoman kissed him. And he forgot that he was but a child in his mother's lap…

The next day, Sagui didn't sell any fruit. But his friends

went door to door as usual.

"Want some oranges? Ten *tostões* a dozen…"

"They're probably stolen…"

Gaitinhas would always blush, while the others protested.

"I'm no thief. I bought them in Areias."

Guedelhas would walk three kilometres of road each morning to sell all the fruit in another village. Later, he'd go train with rag balls, as he was convinced that they'd soon give him a spot at the sports club. The others would either tag along or play quoits at Mirante.

It was there that Sagui—embarrassed and with dark circles under his eyes—spoke to them.

"I didn't sell anythin' today…"

"You sick, pal?"

"No. Some guys were pokin' around the chapel."

The gang got spooked.

"Did they say anything to you?"

"Just asked if I lived there. Best we stash the oranges somewhere else."

"Where?"

"At Zé Vicente's tilery."

"Are you nuts? Any day now they'll be going there to ready the kiln…"

Gineto put an end to the discussion. "We'll move them tonight. Done."

"Better do it in daylight," Sagui countered. "If those guys are onto us, they might show up again tonight."

Gineto began doubting the clumsy excuse of his smaller friend. *Another tall tale*, he thought. He followed Sagui's steps all afternoon. He saw him enter the chapel carrying mysterious bundles, then run through the streets as if looking for someone. Caught up in the chase, Gineto hid behind some stones among the ruins, and while he waited, he found himself wishing he were a law enforcer more than a fruit thief. A law enforcer like the King of the Cowboys[38], who took justice into his own hands in the movies.

But then Sagui showed up with the Madwoman, who was laughing and gesturing. Astonished, Gineto nearly let out a whistle. He hadn't seen that coming. *That guy! Hanging around with the Madwoman, and not saying a word to his friends…* He chuckled. *And he's eating the gang's oranges with her!*

He couldn't rest until he confronted Sagui.

"So, you big phony! You've been messin' around with the Madwoman, and come here tryin' to fool us?"

"Me?!"

"Don't play dumb. I saw you two at the chapel."

For a moment, Sagui was at a loss.

"I was afraid you'd hurt her… She's actually kind of pitiful. Sometimes she doesn't even seem crazy."

"I just wanna have some fun too, you know…" Gineto said impatiently.

"But don't tell the others…"

"Not a word."

A week later, the entire gang was spending their business earnings on gifts for the Madwoman.

Life had never been so good for them. Not even when the first autumn rains signalled a break from toil at the tilery and the coming fun at the Fair.

Gaitinhas no longer handed over the money from the oranges to his mother, and he'd sneak out of the house to avoid her scolding and complaints.

"You're not working now, João?"

He'd lower his eyes in shame and lie, "The work's finished…"

"If only I could get out of bed… Poor Ti Rosa, she's spent a fortune on us."

She'd cough, and then wouldn't have the heart to send her son out begging.

He'd feel sorry for her and swear to himself he'd mend his ways. But the moment he reached the chapel, he'd forget his mother's sad face and weary voice.

"Gaitinhas, go get some wine."

"Only if you give me a cigarette…"

The others would also help themselves to the pack that Gineto had somehow gotten his hands on.

"And matches? Gaitinhas, bring us a box."

They'd empty their pockets and drain the wine bottle, too.

"Pirica's a real soak…"

"Well, all men drink."

Faced with that argument, the others would hush and drink too. Then, they'd deal cards and pass the time playing *bisca*[39] while the Madwoman was out on her dizzy strolls through the village. Thus the raids on the estates dwindled. Only when they ran out of money—and even then, grudgingly—would they bring themselves to crawl through the damp grass of the orange groves. Other than that, only the Madwoman could draw them away from there.

One night, Sagui burst in, out of breath and barely able to speak.

"Guess what? Some guy smacked the Madwoman and dragged her away."

"When?"

"Just now, over at the tavern."

They immediately dropped the cards and went after the man, until they found him near the inlets.

"Hey! Let the Madwoman go!" Gineto demanded, after the others had formed a circle. Just a few steps away, the man sized up his foes like a cornered wolf. Pirica took cover behind Gaitinhas, who was shaking with fear before this seemingly unbeatable giant. But Gineto, springing like a fish, slammed a fierce headbutt to the man's chest, knocking him into the water.

Meanwhile, the Madwoman had gotten away, stumbling as she went. And the boys, like rabbits, scurried back to their chapel hideout.

The adventure fueled laughs and jokes for days on end. They drank to Gineto, who knocked men down just like Tom Mix. And on Sunday, they went to the movies to see themselves in the hero.

They pooled their money in front of a massive poster plastered on the wall, which showed a cowboy—red kerchief flapping in the wind and a revolver on his belt—riding a spirited horse rearing up over a hair-raising gorge. After a lot of sounding it out, Gaitinhas informed them it was Tim Macacoi[40], starring in *Fearless Rider*[41].

"I like Tom Mix better," Gineto said. But Guedelhas swore

the film was amazing.

Behind them, other kids were eagerly listening to their remarks.

"Let me in with you, Gineto," one of them pleaded.

"The usher won't let you…"

Pirica noticed the kid's scrawny little body and joked, "Carry him on your shoulders."

The cinema bell drowned out the laughter of some and the disappointment of others. People were arriving. Near the second poster, boys in ties were debating Greta Garbo's beauty. Ladies passed by, trailing perfumes that the boys' noses eagerly inhaled.

"What a sweet smell, eh!"

"Please give me a ticket…"

"Get lost, kid!"

The guard came over and ordered the crowd to clear the way so Arturinho could enter, followed by Mr. Castro and his mommy.

"Please, a ticket…" Coca repeated.

"I'm only five *tostões* short…"

"Back off!" the guard barked. "This is no place for begging. I want the entrance clear."

The street kids, standing in a semicircle, kept pestering passersby. One of them boldly tried to sneak in between the legs of the people entering, but the guard dragged him back out to the street by his ears.

Gineto's group approached too, making a ruckus.

"Quiet down!" one of the ushers yelled. "You'll all end up in jail if you keep this up."

"We got tickets."

"Then come in. Hey... not you. You're not wearing a jacket."

"I don't need a jacket for the gallery. Let me in..."

"I said no."

Gineto turned back, fuming. He thought of the blue suit his father had promised him in the winter, and tears of rage welled up in his eyes. If the guard hadn't been standing there with a pistol at his side, he would've gone in, even if it meant forcing his way through with his pocketknife.

The scrawny kid tapped him on the shoulder. "I'll lend you this jacket, Gineto. But you gotta tell me the story after, 'kay?"

He promised he would. The jacket looked like a *campino's*[42] smock on him, but he showed up at the cinema entrance as if holding a box seat ticket in his hand. The ushers laughed. And his buddies, inside, found an excuse for their first uproar—one that, despite calls for silence, only ended when Gaitinhas and others began reading the subtitles aloud so the illiterate in the audience could follow along.

It was a monotonous murmur descending from the gallery to the general admission area, just in front of the main seats.

"Slower!" shouted a boy who struggled with reading.

Even Gaitinhas, captivated by the images and music, was beginning to lose his reputation as a scholar.

"Why aren't you readin', Gaitinhas?"

"The movie's going too fast..."

Little by little, antsy for the cowboys to show up, the boys lost interest in Greta Garbo. They couldn't understand why that shameless courtesan—who'd already kissed Armand Duval ten times right there in front of everyone—was now turning down the young man's love. That's why Gineto started acting up in the gallery, prompting a wave of protest from the teary-eyed ladies who were weeping as though they were Marguerite Gautier themselves.

Out on the street, the scrawny kid who'd lent the jacket was shivering with cold. Coca was pestering latecomers, pleading, "Let me in with you. Please."

When the film ended, the boys tossed around crude remarks and picked better seats. Gaitinhas hid behind them so that Arturinho, all prim in his box seat, wouldn't see the holes in his suit. He had half a mind to mess up the boy's sleek hair with one of the paper balls Gineto was throwing from the gallery. But the lights went out, and Tim McCoy was greeted with rounds of applause.

The murmur returned, like a litany of the faithful. Now everyone understood why the cowboy had rescued the girl from the stagecoach bandits. Gineto thought of Rosete, and his pals yearned for the Madwoman. Every so often, applause and enthusiastic shouts erupted, which the street kids outside could hear through the closed doors.

The climactic moment was coming—the hero was about to face off with the bandit leader. The boys squirmed in their seats and held their breath. Gaitinhas bit his nails and, not knowing why, found himself rooting for the bandits, unlike Sagui, who couldn't take his eyes off the cowboy. The cowboy strode down the street, the villain waiting at the corner, gun in hand. One more step and it would be certain death… In a panic, Sagui stood up on his seat and let out a yell that echoed through the entire cinema: "Watch out, Macacoi! The guy's at the corner!"

Right after that, applause and whistles thundered through the room, as the bandit had been defeated. And the boy smiled for having warned the Fearless Rider just in time.

✦ ✦ ✦

THOSE were golden days. There were oranges to sell and the promise of other kinds of fruit on the valley's trees. The bad weather was gone. The boys breathed in the purer, warmer air as if spring were bringing life anew. The Madwoman stilled the sap that bubbled in their blood, and the gentle shade of the chapel ruins banished the living shadows of home from their minds.

But one day, the Madwoman vanished without a trace. In the orchards, the oranges were harvested. And the gang slipped back to a life of uncertainty on the sad, lightless streets. Gineto went back to scaring little kids with his mischief, toppling boats in the ditches, knocking down stone castles, and lashing out at random.

"Leave the little ones alone," Gaitinhas would scold. But Gineto ignored every such plea.

Guedelhas went back to soccer practice, eager for the job that was slow in coming. And Pirica, with languor, took to mindless drinking, to drown his longing for the Madwoman.

II

MAQUINETA ARRIVED, panting and hopping with excitement, and burst out, waving his arms in joy, "Hey guys! Tomorrow's the day… Tomorrow…"

He caught his breath.

"Tomorrow, what?" Gaitinhas asked.

"I got a job! I'm gonna work with the machines!"

His weasel face lit up with a wide grin of pride and joy.

"At the Great Factory?" the other boy pressed.

Without waiting for an answer, Sagui chimed in, "Let him talk. It's a load of bunk."

"On my life, it's true."

He swore it because he was telling the truth.

"Hey, Gineto! Maquineta's gonna work at the Factory."

The shout echoed through the sleepy street.

"What the…"

The boys dropped their tip-cat sticks, then formed a tight circle around their friend. Maquineta stood there with a silly grin on his crooked mouth, beaming with pride as he relished the moment. How many years had he waited for this! Now they wouldn't mock him anymore.

But the gang pressed closer, jostling. Questions rained down.

"Alright, quit yappin'," Gineto ordered. "Let him speak."

They fell silent, and Maquineta told his story: "My mom had put in the request ages ago. She even went straight to the director, it seems… No—actually, she spoke to his wife."

He paused to reconsider. He didn't know anything else… there wasn't really much of a story to it. Or maybe he just lacked Sagui's knack for storytelling.

"The point is that Má-Cara[43] sent word for me to show up tomorrow," he finished in one breath.

"And it's really a job at the machines?" Pirica asked, bitter with envy.

"Of course. My mom even said I had a talent for metalwork…"

He looked around at his friends' faces. No, this time nobody was laughing.

He sat down on a doorstep, and the others followed suit. Gineto lit a scraggly cigarette stub.

"And how much will you make?" he asked.

"Ah, that I don't know. Maybe ten *mil-réis.*"

"Man, what luck!" Gaitinhas muttered, head down, as he thought about what he could do with ten *mil-réis* a day.

"That's six and a half *mil-réis* more than at the tilery," Sagui added.

Silence fell. The boys' aspirations were being stoked once again—they'd been dashed a thousand times before. And sadness settled over the group, stealing away any room for dreams. Little by little, their confidence in the job requests they each had made at the Great Factory was fading away. The gang felt defeated.

Gineto had set the rule: "What's for one is for all." Now, sucking on his cigarette butt, he thought bitterly: *Hunger for all—except one.*

It was the first defection.

Maquineta was sad now too and at a loss for words. Trying to break the mood, Gaitinhas joked, "Aren't you going to treat us to something?"

The others laughed, and their friend perked up.

"Of course I'll treat you. Once I get my first pay, we'll all go to Ramadas."

"To Ramadas? You wish…"

Maquineta clammed up. Only the boys who worked—those who were like men—got into the best tavern in town.

Embarrassed, he got up. "See you later. I'm gonna go get my things ready for tomorrow," he mumbled as an excuse.

And off he went down the street, with nothing to get ready.

Silence returned. Evening fell. The houses' shadows crept forward timidly and erased the forgotten circles that coarse hands had drawn in the street with tip-cat sticks.

✦ ✦ ✦

MAQUINETA couldn't sleep. His mother had told him, "Go to bed, Toino. Work starts at six o'clock."

He'd gone to bed. By the light of a candle stub, his mother was sewing buttons onto his best outfit—the one he'd first worn three years before at the Fair. And Maquineta was thinking: *Do the boots still fit? I can't go barefoot to the workshops. Too bad I don't have coveralls. Or a wrench belt, like metalworkers wear…*

Never mind. A month from now… He started doing the math in his head, but couldn't work out the numbers. *Will I really earn ten mil-réis?* Doubts suddenly crept into his mind: *Why the hell do they start at six o'clock? Does Má-Cara run the workshops too?*

"Hey Mom, what's Má-Cara's name?"

"It's Enriques."

The boy kept untangling his thoughts. *I'll get there and say, 'Mr. Anriques, I'm the boy the director's wife said to be assigned to the workshops.' The guy ought to welcome me. After all, it was the boss's wife who put in the request.*

His mother blew out the candle stub, which was about to burn out, so he'd have light to get dressed at dawn. The darkness brought more cold to the miserable hovel. Above his head, Maquineta felt his mother groping around the cot. He lay there still dreaming, his soul awake to the thrill of that one-of-a-kind day. Moments later, he had the impression that the rhythmic sound of the machines was already caressing his ears, just like the mournful *fados* that Gaitinhas had picked up from the tavern radio. What sweet music! And he fell asleep, lulled by the whistling wind that lingered outside.

Deep into the night, Maquineta woke with a start, his eyes wide open to the darkness of the room. He was about to get up, but his mother calmed him. "It's still early, Toino. Sleep."

He wrapped himself again in the patchwork blanket. *What time is it?* It seemed to him that time itself had fallen asleep. But after a while...

"Son! Hey, Toino, it's time!"

He jumped out of bed. Putting on his unused boots was a struggle. *But in the workshops,* he thought, *there won't be much walking around.*

"See you later, Mom."

"Your lunch is on the shelf."

That's right—he'd forgotten the chunk of dry bread.

He went out. In the sky, the stars twinkled with sleepiness. The sun had to be somewhere beyond the river, casting colour over the drowsy heath. But inside Maquineta, a dawn of joy had already broken.

At the factory gate, a group of men stood talking in low voices. They had weathered faces and gloomy eyes, and angular bodies worn down by weariness that never quite left them. They were waiting for their own dawn...

A figure appeared behind the gate's bars.

"You can come in."

It was Má-Cara.

Standing farther back, Maquineta waited for the men to pass through the gate. He was about to speak.

"Mister..." He shuddered. He couldn't recall the name. "Má-Cara... Má-Cara... Damn it!" he muttered nervously.

"So, you coming in or staying put? You're starting early with the stalling," the foreman barked.

Maquineta followed behind the others. *Má-Cara... Mister...* How infuriating!

They took down his name and handed him a basket, while he kept trying to remember the man's name. The group stopped at the far end of the factory, by the river. Maquineta gathered his courage.

"What's that guy's name?" he whispered to the worker closest to him, pointing to the foreman.

The other man gave him a mocking grin.

"What, you don't know? That's Má-Cara."

Just then, the foreman's voice boomed with authority: "Hey! You lot with the baskets. Down this plank, up that one, and dump the coal into the carts." He made a sweeping gesture of command. "Come on, line up."

That's when reality hit Maquineta. He cast a bewildered, questioning glance around him, as if searching for the illusion that had slipped away. The machines were behind him now, in the shadowy sheds that loomed like fortress walls. Their symphony of motors, of hammers and anvils, of belts and drums didn't reach him here. This was the factory's forsaken dock. Choppy water under makeshift piers; dark boats without sail rocking side by side in the wash, their hulls swollen with sooty cargo. In the distance was the misty plain, and nearby, the indifferent, sleepwalking river. The landscape: solitude.

Maquineta was about to look back once more at the distant factory, but the worker behind him shoved him toward the pier. "Move it, boy!"

The unloading began. Basket emptied, basket filled… Legs buckled under heavy loads; nimble feet moved carefully along the plank, because one misstep meant a dangerous fall—the human hustle went on and on. On the pier, the foreman kept watch over the unloading; in the boats, his trusted men didn't let the shovels rest.

"I want those baskets packed and moving!"

Basket emptied, basket filled… The carts rolled along the tracks and the coal was already piling up in the yard.

"Hey you! Damn show-pony! What are you waiting for?"

The mocking shout was aimed at Maquineta. *Show-pony…*

He hadn't even thought to take off his jacket, the one he'd first worn three years before at the Fair. Now, smudged and tattered, it bunched around his arms and made him look like a scarecrow.

Basket emptied, basket filled... Maquineta shuffled back and forth, panting and sweating. He was careful with his feet on the plank, because his boots—besides pinching his toes—slipped like he was walking on grease.

At the factory, the whistle blew long. Eight o'clock. Maquineta's heart beat harder under his aching chest. The workshop guys would be starting now.

I'll go to him and say, 'Mr. Anriques, I'm the boy that the boss's wife recommended...' That's right. The foreman's name is Anriques. But it was no use remembering that now.

Má-Cara noticed the young worker's slumping posture and lashed out at him, "You damn slug! You're already behind a full run. You're sleeping on the job, but I see everything."

Not satisfied with that, he turned to the men on the boat. "Handle this kid's basket. Load it up heavy, you hear?"

Maquineta cast a pleading look at the men with the shovels. But they were the foreman's trusted men—they knew their boss was keeping watch... And so the boy, humiliated and defeated, feeling all alone among all those people who couldn't see his knack for metalwork, let the tears draw long streaks down his soot-smudged face.

A fellow worker tapped him on the shoulder. "Don't cry, boy! Look, the guy's laughing at you."

Maquineta braced himself and clenched his lips. *I won't give him reasons to mock me, even if it kills me...* But the baskets were getting heavier and heavier. He couldn't tell anymore whether the drops running down his face were tears or sweat. The foreman was laughing on the pier... while his feet were in agony, like prisoners in his boots—just like he was a prisoner under Má-Cara's predatory gaze.

He rolled up his jacket into a cushion and took off one boot before they could shove another basket at him. But the men's arms moved like machine pistons.

"Hurry up, boy..."

Off he went, up the plank—one foot bare, the other shod—under the foreman's taunts, which were harder to bear than the load itself. His thoughts drifted to the high whistle that marked the end of hard labour at the factory, that now had forgotten about him down there by the river. As if time itself were another Má-Cara ruling over that endless grind.

And that barge—it was bottomless! *But I won't fold, even if it kills me,* he thought. He imagined how, at the end of work, he'd stomp the basket into the ground. Then, he'd walk tall past the foreman, as if his body still had strength to spare, and spit on the ground in contempt.

The voice of command cracked through the air like a whip. "Quit the chatter! Get moving."

But the scolding wasn't meant for him. If he had opened his mouth, it would be only to scream his rage against everything and everyone. So he bit his lips and kept probing the barge's hold, which was always dark and offered no hope. Má-Cara had been down there too, piercing the darkness with his feline glare, and had gone back up with the air of a conqueror. One more basket, then another...

"Knock off!"

Maquineta stood there, with his arm still raised to hold the basket on his back, as if he hadn't heard.

"What, feeling strong now? Drop that basket."

He looked the foreman square in the eye. His dry, parched mouth didn't let him spit on the ground in contempt. He tried to straighten his exhausted body... He faltered. The basket slipped from his hands... His legs carried him toward the exit gate...

And it was his mother who collected the day's wages, later on.

III

GAITINHAS HADN'T SET foot on the street for two days, not since the doctor had come to examine his mother at Rosa's urging. He'd waited for the doctor to scribble a prescription on paper that he could then dash to the pharmacy to get filled. But the doctor shook his head twice and left the way he came. Ti Rosa hid her tears in her apron, and Gaitinhas sensed that something terrible was about to happen.

His mother's face was paler than the bedsheets. She coughed constantly, and her slender, almost translucent hands could barely lift the handkerchief to her mouth. Only her eyes still held that same wet gleam of fever and sorrow.

"Do you want some soup, Madalena?"

She said no in a barely audible voice.

"I'll be back at five. But if you need me, João should come get me."

At the door, she warned, "Don't leave her side, child."

Gaitinhas sat down in front of his mother, whose deep gaze shifted between him and Pedro's portrait. Silence, inside their home and out on the street. The whole alley held its breath in the face of that slow agony, and even the sun, pale and mournful, came to lean over the eaves.

"João…"

The boy leaned against the straw bed. Was his mother going to talk to him about work? Maybe Ti Rosa, who'd seen him selling oranges, had told her about his running around with Gineto.

"I'm going to leave you, my son. You're a man now…"

The coughing choked her words. She tried again: "Try to find work. Your father will come back one day…"

Her eyes turned to the portrait of the man she'd never see again, and she wept.

"Tell him…"

Once more, the coughing tore away scraps of life from her. Gaitinhas collapsed beside her, his head buried in the bed clothes, sobbing like when he was a child. "*You're a man now…*" He'd heard those words once before, on an autumn day, when he'd also cried in despair at not being able to go back to school. His boots had worn out beyond repair—he didn't even know where they'd ended up. Later came the begging, then stealing fruit from Arturinho's orchard. "*You're a man now… You can help your mother.*" But he hadn't helped her, nor had he become a man, because there he was, crying—and Gineto always said that a man never cries, not even if it kills him. He'd spent his money on gifts for the Madwoman—and here was his mother right beside him, dying…

He cried harder, though his mother's fingers over his hair were a gesture of blessing and forgiveness. But so light was her touch that even that caress dissolved into his deep sorrow. When he lifted his head, his mother was still, eyes closed, as if asleep. He tiptoed away. Across from him, on the grimy wall, it seemed to him that his father's eyes, carrying the same sorrow, followed him throughout the house, perhaps demanding an account of the money he'd so carelessly spent…

He changed his mind and moved around. He began

studying the shapes that time had created on the walls' peeling plaster. He'd first noticed the largest one, which resembled a horse, when he'd been sick with measles. It was a horse like the one stranded in the fields during the floods... His gaze shifted to another shape. But his thoughts returned to the fields, where the frog from the High Farm croaked ominously, and his street buddies turned over bodies, searching for Malesso. Those corpses with waxen faces and purple lips like...

He stifled a scream of terror. Had his mother died? His body was seized with tremors and soft sobs. *And Ti Rosa still hasn't come back!* he thought.

When the factory whistle blew, it was as if his mother had suddenly been cured.

Rosa Coxa entered quietly.

"Well?"

"She seems to be sleeping..."

The old woman approached, placed her hand on Madalena's icy forehead, and broke into deep sobs—as if she'd just lost a daughter.

✦ ✦ ✦

SHE WAS BURIED the following afternoon, with Ti Rosa limping behind the coffin and her son's friends following along. The sun had hidden itself behind a cloud. And Maquineta didn't show up either, because he'd been avoiding everyone since leaving the factory. It was an obscure funeral, like the life that had ended.

Ti Rosa had made the rounds at the looms, bag in hand,

as was her custom. She only had to change two words: "For Madalena, who died yesterday."

"She died? Poor thing!"

"Oh, it's the living who suffer," lamented a thin girl who had three little children.

"We complain, but…"

The lint from the wool tangled their voices and stirred stubborn coughs in their chests. And the foreman's gaze, even from afar, cut off conversations and kept the looms moving.

With Coca's help, Gaitinhas had also gone around the village with half a sheet of notebook paper in hand.

"Please spare a little something for my mother's burial…" he said, showing everyone the donation list.

On their return from the cemetery, Rosa Coxa gathered up Madalena's few belongings, which weren't even enough to cover the overdue house rent, and said to Gaitinhas, "You're like a grandson to me now. You'll come live with me, alright?"

He didn't know how to answer. Silent and sad, he followed behind her, his thoughts in disarray. He refused supper. And in the darkness of night, he drenched the unfamiliar pillow with tears.

Days went by without him showing up to see his friends. He'd go to the lookout at Mirante, like when he was little, and stay there watching time drift by and the taut-sailed boats glide past. Now more than ever, he longed to sail away on a boat like that to search for his father, who was as far away as a dream.

Gineto was growing desperate. "Maquineta's gone, Gaitinhas is in mourning… Damn it all!"

"There's no oranges left now either…"

"No oranges? Just yesterday I saw two orange trees loaded with fruit in Castro's garden."

"Get real. With the house and the dog right next to it, who's gonna risk going in?"

"I would. The point is you guys would have to help."

Sagui couldn't muster the courage to cheer up his friend. Spring had sparked other yearnings in him, a new direction for his life. He was sick and tired of begging for alms and selling fruit door to door, which was just another form of begging. Like the others, he sometimes felt gripped by an inexplicable sadness, only to shake it off later, but feeling even more dissatisfied than before.

"One of these days, I'm gettin' outta here."

"And go where?"

"Who knows…? Down some road or other, to see the world."

"Goin' back to the circus, eh?"

Memories of his tormented childhood came to his mind, and he fell silent while scratching indecipherable doodles on the ground.

"Don't fret. The tileries will start up soon."

"That can't come soon enough."

And the tileries rose in his thoughts like a kind of deliverance.

✦ ✦ ✦

ROSA COXA repeated that misfortunes never come alone. Other women wept. That day, the piercing chorus of the factory whistles wasn't accompanied by the weavers' usual chatter at quitting time. They lingered in the courtyard in silent groups, with some of them still hoping for a countermand.

"Are you leaving or not?" the gatekeeper asked aloud. "Looks like you lot want to sleep here tonight… Are you staying with me, Luísa?"

But none of the women found it funny. They filed out like a funeral procession, wiping their bitterness on the ends of their blue smocks. Bits of wool fluff in their hair made their premature aging all the more visible.

"What's going to become of us now? A full week's pay wasn't enough to get me by, let alone three days…"

"It won't even cover my house rent."

"At least you got your man bringing in some money. But me…"

"We should go talk to the manager," Maria do Bote suggested. "He wouldn't lay us all off."

"What good would that do? They say it's due to the war…"

"Who knows? But we can't live like this."

Still, determined to somehow get by, they returned home.

Maria do Bote opened the door to her house, and everything inside seemed gloomier and barer than usual. Only the alarm clock atop the worm-eaten dresser flaunted its shine, ticking away in a steady rhythm through hours it could never live. She looked at it with melancholy, as if it were a useless trinket. Then, with sudden resolve, she tucked it under her shawl and headed to Rodrigues's office.

At the entrance, she hesitated. But the pawnbroker approached at once with eager charm.

"Please come in. At your service, madam." He rubbed his covetous hands together.

"Mr. Rodrigues, I've brought something…" She carefully set the nickel-plated clock on the desk and added, "I'd like to pawn it, but just for a short while."

The pawnbroker grinned. "And how much are you looking to get for this, ma'am?"

"I don't know, Mr. Rodrigues. Maybe twenty *escudos*…"

"Come on, now. This thing's worthless. You'd have been better off bringing clothes."

"Worthless?! It cost me thirty-five *mil-réis.*"

"I'll give you five *escudos,* if you want. And that's doing you a big favor, mind you."

"Hard times for those in need…" Maria do Bote sighed.

She looked once more at her precious clock, listened to its melodious ticking, and left with five *escudos* in her pocket and tears in her eyes.

When she got home, Gineto asked her, "Where's the clock, Mom?"

"I got rid of it. Work at the factory is down to three days per week now, and your father spends all he earns on wine…"

Gineto noticed the despondency in her voice and the deeper wrinkles on her face.

"Don't worry," he said. "I'll find a way to earn something."

That night, when everyone was fast asleep, he snuck out to raid the orange trees at the High Farm all by himself.

Days later, also in the dead of night, Deolinda—fed up with her mother's nagging and her father's drinking—left home and ran to her boyfriend's arms. The neighbours whispered,

"Would you look at that! A little brat like her… Before long she'll have a whole litter of kids and not even the breast milk to feed them."

But Maria do Bote didn't cry for sorrow. It was bound to happen, sooner or later… And the girl wasn't even bringing in enough to cover for the food she ate.

It was her father who, out of grief, drank himself into a stupor that nearly killed him.

GAITINHAS watched Rosa Coxa wrap her shawl around herself and head out. *She's going begging,* he thought. And here he was, eating her soup, living easy. No—he had to follow through on the idea that had been bubbling in his head. Everything there felt foreign and heavy to him. The old woman was always sighing now, as if dragging around a great burden. She often spoke of her late friend. "Your mother…" And if that happened while he was eating, he'd lose his appetite.

So, after much thinking, he grabbed a pencil and wrote a note that he'd leave on the table, where it could easily be seen:

"Ti Rosa, don't be angry. I'm going away. Thank you for everything. Someday I'll pay you back.

João da Fonseca."

And because he'd forgotten that Ti Rosa couldn't read, he felt at ease when he left to go live with Sagui in the chapel ruins.

IV

HE WANDERED through the rubble with his hands behind his back and his head hanging low. The workyard was covered in white and yellow flowers; the ponds had turned into lakes; and in the inlets' uncultivated land, clumps of reed had spread. But to Zé Vicente, spring only meant expenses. The kilns were on the verge of collapse, the clay pits had been laid to waste, and there was debris everywhere. *And Mr. Castro's waiting...* he thought.

His father had left him all this in the golden days, and he'd fancied himself a lord. Sporting a white jacket and a Mazzantini-style[45] hat, he rode a Hispano-Arab horse that stirred envy at the bull parades, and mingled with gentry and landowners. He never missed a branding or a bullfight. With no thought for the future, he'd fathered five children with the woman he'd chosen, after many escapades with chorus girls and prostitutes. He'd counted on the tilery being a goldmine that would never run out. There was no better tile in the whole country!

The boys would toil from sunup to sundown for a crust of bread, and the main inlet was a dock teeming with boats all year long. Not even the Great Factory, right next door, could cast a shadow over his business in those days. Perhaps he hadn't noticed it. Just like he hadn't noticed the French tile factories flooding the markets and steering the boats to other places.

But the tilery was a goldmine only until the cement block outpaced the brick and the eight-hour workday law—one of the Republic's many shams, as he used to say—crippled production.

Lost in these memories, Zé Vicente walked around the tilery and stopped beside the skeletal white horse prancing by the river's edge, in a daze caused by the sun and the grass it hadn't seen in months. Of his beasts of burden, he had only that one left, the sorriest of the lot. And on the storage sheds, only a few rows of bricks remained—barely enough to barter for a boatload of firewood.

And I still haven't paid the rent... he thought. He set off for the High Farm. Once there, he said, "Mr. Castro... I'm ashamed to even..."

"Have a seat, Zé Vicente."

He sank his thin body into the armchair and resumed his plea. "... I'm ashamed to even come here. You know it's been a rough year. For everyone, of course," he added, wringing his hands and his wits.

The armchair was the problem—deep and wide, it nearly brought his knees up to his chin.

Surely Mr. Castro would interrupt his justification at any moment. *"Rough year, no doubt..."* But the landlord remained silent and smiling in front of him.

I'm in luck, Zé Vicente thought. He cleared his throat and continued: "The storm knocked the whole place down, as you surely know. Of the stacks I'd stored there—some thirty thousand bricks—I couldn't salvage even half. Just imagine the loss I took, Mr. Castro! But now, with people needing bricks for walls and chimneys that the wind tore up..."

The landowner's smile faded, perhaps as he thought of his

own losses at the Islet, and Zé Vicente took that for annoyance.

"I know that you have nothing to do with my troubles, sir…"

"Oh, please. You're just laying out your case, Zé Vicente. Of course, if I can help… You know that I'm your friend."

"Thank you so much. I haven't forgotten that I already fell behind the past two years, and that you were kind enough to wait, sir. That's exactly why it was so hard for me to come here. I was counting on getting back on my feet with a few deals…"

"But… Come on, you ought to have made some money anyway. Bricks went up in price…"

"They didn't go up at all, Mr. Castro."

He paused and adjusted his body in the armchair, while the landlord lit a cigar.

"My colleagues and I had agreed to raise brick prices and put an end to undercutting. One day, I put in a bid to supply bricks for a factory being built in Póvoa, and Meneses goes and makes them an offer of ten *mil-réis* cheaper per thousand. That scoundrel, eh? From then on, the price has only gone down."

"Good grief!" Mr. Castro exclaimed with feigned astonishment.

"The only thing saving him is that I've got five kids to raise. If I didn't need the tilery, like he doesn't need his…"

He choked back his anger in fear of going too far. Meneses was a friend of Mr. Castro's.

"It's not worth losing your head over it, Zé Vicente. Business is business. And those who've got what it takes…"

He made a motion to get up. Zé Vicente also rose from the armchair, not knowing how to bring up the rent again.

Mr. Castro's pointy fingernails dug aggressively into the desk's edge. His mouth, however, kept that same promising smile.

"Well then, if you would be so kind as to give me a little more time, sir…"

"Look, you do what's best for you. It's not that I don't need the rent, obviously. But a delay of a month or so shouldn't be a reason for us to fall out."

"I'm very grateful to you, Mr. Castro."

As he left, it was as if spring had come alive at that very moment.

He saw the fields decked out in green, the sky clear of clouds, and the sun shining, ready to burn. *And people say that Mr. Castro's a miser. Slanderers! Envy, nothing more…* He breathed in the estate's scent deeply, and returned to the tilery in high spirits.

"Hey, Felipe. We need to get things ready. I want this place up and running."

"Already, boss?"

"Don't you see the weather? April's almost over."

"We're still gonna get a lot of rain."

"Do as I say."

The foreman made a mutt-like face, but still dared to grumble, "First we have to fix the kiln. It's in a sorry state."

"People will be coming to help tomorrow. And if the season goes well, you can count on having bricks to patch up your house. But I want a firm hand, all right?"

"Don't worry, boss." Felipe thanked him and walked away.

Zé Vicente remained at the kiln, leaning against the stair railing as he reviewed his plans: *That bit of money I was going to* use to keep the landlord off my back will be enough for a boatload of firewood. But what of the horse? That nag wouldn't survive working the mill. The leftover bricks from last year should be enough to trade for a mule… That scoundrel Meneses! And some people hate Mr. Castro. What a bunch!

The afternoon was fading away. A gentle breeze from the north stirred the stagnant water in the inlets. The tenant cast his eyes around the tilery and thought further: *I'll tell the ditch diggers to come—they'll pay their own way, of course—and get this place going by the end of May.*

✦ ✦ ✦

THE DITCH diggers boarded the mail train at Alfarelos, after a full day of preparations and reminders.

"Take your wool socks."

"What for?"

"It will be cold come September, dear."

"That's a long way off…"

They made a final round of the fields. Their hearts would pine for them.

"Don't forget to sulphur the vineyard, you hear?"

"Just go and don't worry about it."

Rita Pinta came to the station to pass along messages for her husband. "Tell him I'm worried sick about him. And that our boy has started talking. We miss him terribly…"

"Make sure you write to me, Arlindo," another girl whimpered.

"So long as you remember me."

Moved, she turned her face away.

"Come on, Micas. This time's the last, you know that."

He'd said the same one year prior, and the year before that. Just like the train's rattle was always the same as it came and went: *"pouca terra, pouca terra..."*[46] The train spoke the truth. Not owning a scrap of land he could stick a hoe in was why he was in that third-class carriage, surrounded by blankets, ditching spades, and patched-up sacks. Because in summer, life was rough for everyone, and women's arms were enough for the available work in the fields. But those who had land of their own managed better.

"You look kinda down, Arlindo."

"Just thinkin' about a small plot for corn..."

"Don't worry, the girl's old man will give you her hand anyway."

"That's what you say. Been at this fool's game for five years now... And if it don't work out this time, I'm done with the tilery."

The oldest of the bunch chuckled. "I've been sayin' that for thirty years—and here I am."

The train, with its beat-up racket, scoffed at their talk and yearnings. *"Pouca terra, pouca terra..."* And the diggers' dreams faded behind them, like the landscape sliding past the window: cornfields, waterwheels pulling up buckets, white houses nestled among pine trees... Fleeting images these men's eyes didn't need to linger on. They had carried them in their minds since the cradle. That's why the first few leagues of the journey were a heavy, gloomy vertigo.

"How 'bout we eat somethin'?" one of them suggested.

"Good call. I got some fine grub here…"

They opened their bags to kill their hunger and pass the time.

"Is it still long before we get there, Dad?"

"Don't bug me about how far it is. Seems like you're itchin' to grab a shovel…"

The boy turned away from the window, which the night had slowly darkened, and stretched out on the bench. *I wanted to go on this journey so bad, and it turns out it's nothing like I'd dreamed,* he thought. The benches, harder and narrower than reclining chairs, wore down his body. And on the ceiling, the dim bulb brought to mind the flickering embers of a fireplace.

I wish we were there already. He shut his eyes and fell asleep, until his father gave him a rough shake.

"Blasted boy—didn't even mind the makeshift bed."

"He might even like sleeping in the quarters…"

"Quarters, Dad?"

The foreman smiled.

"Don't worry, you're not goin' off to be a soldier. Quarters is what we call the place where we sleep."

The train eased into a slower pace. Morning was breaking, and the sun was trying out new colours over the plains. Shadows melted into the quiet, sleepy river, which looked like a stretch of road with no trees for shelter.

The ditch diggers thought of the Mondego[47] caressing the poplar groves and corn fields—a mirror for their yearnings. And when they stepped off the train, their hands were firmly gripping the shovels that churned up the inlets and their ambitions alike.

SUMMER

I

THE FISHING BOATS extinguish their lights. Then—oars moving like giant bird wings—they pull up to the edges of the inlets as the water recedes. They're darker than the night, as dark as the lives of those who toil in them night and day.

The fishermen drive two stakes as gnarled as their own hands into the mud, at the bow and stern of the boats, and go to sleep under the tarpaulin covering, dreaming of fish they didn't catch.

In the ashen sky, only the morning star is shining. Keeping it company are the Great Factory's lights, worn out from watching over men and machines for so long.

Though there's still only a hint of morning, in the quarters, the alarm clock has already announced the day. The ditch diggers rise from bunks too hard to soothe weary bodies; they grope for their shovels in the corner; and after fooling their mouths with a chunk of bread harder than the bunks, they head out toward the inlet.

"Let's get to it before the tide rises."

Their legs slide through knee-deep mud and shiver from

the dampness. *Thunk... Thunk...* The first shovel strikes meet solid ground. Their bodies, in a line, make swift movements broken only by the torpor of dawn. Thin and slippery, the inlet's silt doesn't yet stick to the shovels.

The shovels land amid the silence, and the plains beyond the river echo them faintly. Arlindo hears the echo and remembers the friend who disappeared during the floods.

"Did you write to Rita Pinta, master?"

"I didn't. Started to, but didn't have the heart to finish it."

The diggers' silhouettes sway in the inlet like the dry reeds surrounding them.

"What if he didn't die?" one of the men ventures.

"Come on now! He was out in the fields and no one's seen him since..."

"Poor Rita. Waiting a whole year... Damn the hour that made him stay in this cursed place."

"That's what happens when you got nothin' of your own."

Arlindo thinks of the plot of land he's been coveting and tightens his grip on the shovel handle. *This year... even if it kills me!*

But the inlet's silt is quickly cleared away, and now the black, dense sludge feels like a layer of glue. The shovels dig deeper and the effort grows; arms lift higher in throwing motions. No one talks anymore, because they open their mouths only to catch their breath or mutter a curse when clods slip loose.

The sun rises, vexing and biting, and Zé Vicente shows up too, casting sharp glances over the inlets. *That boy...*

"You only brought greenhorns this year, master."

"But they get the job done, boss. Worth as much as a

grown man."

The master's words spark fresh energy. The chunks of sludge being flung from the inlet trace wider arcs through the air, like bullets.

If a shovelful slipped now… The master's son shudders at the thought.

For three days now, the boss's glare has bitten into his back more harshly than the sun.

"That boy there, master…"

"He's my son. Been digging ditches since he was little. He's sixteen now…"

Zé Vicente hesitates. *If I could dock just a single* escudo *from these people… That'd be serious money by summer's end.* The master sees right through him and moves his son to softer mud nearby.

"Dig out another stretch here, boy."

His voice is gruff, but his son answers with a grateful look. The boy carves a hole in the mud and water seeps up; he wets his shovel and his hands. The work gets harsher—the sun does too. It glints off the metal blades and the mud being dug; it dizzies. Yet, more than the toil or the sun, it's Zé Vicente's eyes that scorch the entire inlet.

Feeling the weight of his gaze on their sweaty backs, the diggers bend lower and lower, as if begging for shade and mercy. But there and all around, only the boss's frame casts a shadow on the searing earth.

Harnessed to a wagon, the white horse comes galloping at a forced pace to carry off mud that the heat has already cracked. It hadn't had time to nibble all the grass that spring had sprouted in the workyard and embankments, and now, as it trots, its bones look like they might pierce through its skin. It stops at the tip of the inlet and turns its gentle eyes toward the evergreen clumps of sedge, thinking they might be tender grass.

Zé Vicente's voice rings out: "Send a man for the mud!"

The master hesitates. He wants to send his son, who's panting right beside him, but he needs to show that the young ones are as good as men, so he pretends not to notice his boy's pleading eyes.

"Since you're the oldest, you go, Ti Alberto."

The digger pulls his numbed legs out of the muck and, stumbling like a drunkard, heads over to the wagon.

A boat loaded with pine branches comes tacking into the main inlet. Its white sail, billowing on the mast, looks like a flag of peace. But the ditch work goes on under the merciless heat.

"Make the most of it... The tide's coming."

Let it come, the diggers think. That was the only way they'd cool their burning bodies and ease their fatigue. But the tide doesn't come, because the river's stagnant like a marsh. The wind blows against the bar and against the diggers. The water laps at the mud, but does not rise.

"See if you can be done with that inlet today, master."

"We're doing our best..."

"Might be wise to raise a dike before the river floods in."

Zé Vicente walks away. *If I could dock one* escudo *per man... One hundred and twenty days, times six—seven hundred and twenty* escudos... *That's money, alright.*

The master seals off the mouth of the inlet, delaying the water's caress. His son presses his thirsty mouth to a jug, spilling water down his chest.

"That's enough. Try not to drown."

"It's lukewarm…" the boy complains, and he stays there licking his parched lips, thinking of the singing springs back home.

In the factories, the whistles announce noon, calling the men to lunch. But the diggers keep on, because their clock is the sun or the tide.

"It's never gonna rise, the damn thing…"

"It's up two fingers' breadth…"

"Only two?" the master's son insists with dismay. *Wish I could lie down on my bunk already, hard as it is.*

"What now, boy? You wanna make me look bad?"

He wipes his face with the sleeves of his shirt and gets back to work. A thrust on one side, a thrust on the other—and the long, narrow shovel pulls out clods that the digger flings onto the inlet's bank with a twist of his torso as his legs sink deeper into the mud.

In the men's bare chests, the tide of exhaustion rises faster than the water in the river. Arlindo looks around at the steep banks, high as fortress walls, and mumbles, "This isn't an inlet anymore—it's a pit."

"A cemetery grave," says another.

The master offers a word of comfort: "Don't you worry. You'll make it back to your hometown in one piece."

He forces a laugh; the others fall silent. Arlindo stares at the sliver of river in the distance and yearns for the Mondego.

The boss reappears, showing a more cheerful face. *A good day's work today.*

"Break open the dike, master."

The waters surge into the inlet with a gurgle, and the diggers clean their shovels and their numbed legs. Then, in the shade of the shed, they chew their food and pass the wine bottle from hand to hand.

"If you men would like to earn a few extra hours," Zé Vicente proposes, "you could haul mud with handbarrows."

They look at each other, hesitating. The master's son sighs for his bunk.

"Well, I hope you don't take it the wrong way, boss…" the oldest digger says, excusing himself.

"It's up to you. I'm not forcing anyone. It's just that, since I only have one horse, I thought I'd give you this chance."

The master sees in Zé Vicente's eyes the anger his words didn't reveal, and he fears for the boys. *"You only brought greenhorns this year…"* Arlindo thinks of the cornfield and his talk back then. *"This time's the last, you know…"* And dormant energies awaken. They set down their jackets and shovels, and grab the handbarrows. Zé Vicente spurs the horse, as if to instigate the men as well. But their legs, gone numb in the inlet, falter.

"Don't drag your feet now, that won't do…"

They bite back curses and match their steps to the horse as it pulls the rickety wagon in fits and starts.

The afternoon dissolves into colours behind the hills as the diggers return to the quarters, where the oldest of the group is peeling potatoes for supper.

"So you gave out, eh, Ti Alberto?"

"I'm too old to be a pack mule. I'll always be poor, no matter what…"

"Still, we earned an extra four hours."

"Four? Two hours… that's all."

"Come on! Doesn't that work pay double?"

"No. You don't earn more for your trouble," the master replies with a bitter laugh.

The new digger loses his appetite for supper. He stretches out on the bunk and exhales heavily, like the white horse searching for grass at that hour on the bare, solitary yard.

Outside, the others chew on bread and potatoes, and on old dreams, their talk broken by long silences. The wind cools their sweaty backs; the sultry night soothes their weariness as it slowly descends over the valley.

"Hey, boy, aren't you comin' to eat? Cheer up!"

He replies that he has no appetite and keeps his half-closed eyes on the blackened, unplastered walls, from which onions, small bags, and utensils hang in disarray. Old newspapers line a corner where their best clothes await the journey back home; a nauseating smell of sweat and food hangs in the air.

One after another, the diggers lie down side by side on straw mats, in the lodge that was used as a corral in winter. Through the wide-open door, they see the river gleaming like a mirror and the long fingers of the inlets, now transfigured into plots sprouting grain and rice. They close their eyes— they dream. And the moonlight comes gently to chase away shadows and rats.

II

"WHAT'S YOUR NAME?" asked Zé Vicente, holding the time sheets in his hand.

"Sagui."

"That's a nickname. Your real name?"

"Dunno. Everyone just calls me Sagui."

"Have you ever worked at a tilery?"

He nodded yes.

"Then what name did they put down for you in the records?"

"The master at the Big Tilery said I'd be called Toino."

"And how old are you?"

"No idea."

Zé Vicente sized him up from head to toe and wrote: *António Sagui – 11 years old.*" Though it seemed to him the boy was no more than eight.

"Next one. Name…"

"João da Fonseca."

"Age?"

"Going on twelve."

"At last, a know-it-all shows up here. You haven't worked at a tilery yet…"

"No, sir. I went to school."

"That doesn't matter here. Go to the mud grounds and tell the master to give you work."

Gaitinhas took two steps past the door but stopped, feeling unsure. *The mud grounds… The master… How am I supposed to know who that is? And Sagui, that jerk, didn't wait for me.* He approached a man walking across the workyard.

"Excuse me…"

"What are you sniffin' around here for?"

"I'm looking for the master," he stammered.

"I'm the master. Get to work, quick!"

Flushing and trembling, the boy broke into a run without knowing where he was going. In front of the kiln, a line of boys with bundles on their backs blocked his way. As he waited for them to unload the firewood, he heard them mocking the dazed way he was gawking at the tilery.

"Look at that chump…"

"Maybe he thinks he's the boss's son."

One of them brushed a pine branch against his face; another pinched his butt. Gaitinhas was about to strike back at the insult, but the tilery master appeared just then, seething.

"Still here, you little bastard?"

And he gave him a shove. Dumbstruck, the boy stared at him, his lunch bag forgotten in his hand.

"Never seen me before? Get to the inlet."

No. He'd never seen that scorched, wrinkled face in which only one eye glinted—a cruel, sardonic eye.

"If I catch you standing around again! What's your name?"

"João da Fonseca."

The master twisted his face into something like a smile and rasped, "Your nickname, you fool!"

"It's Gaitinhas."

"Got it. Now move it."

He set down his bag in a corner of the kiln and got in line, wanting to cry. Everything there disoriented him. The boss had asked for his name; the master demanded a nickname... His workmates, kids like him, looked anything but friendly; and Sagui had vanished without a trace.

But the foreman cut his thoughts short.

"Get up front..."

He climbed onto the woodpile, which made the boat sway in the inlet's dark water, and grabbed the bundle another boy handed him. His feet were pricked by pine needles and then by thistles along the barely worn path. Dry pine branches scratched his face and neck. *If only I could adjust the bundle...* He was about to slow down, but the boy behind him was already pressing his own load against his back.

"Pick it up, pal. Zarolho's[48] over there watching..."

He quickened his step, biting his lips in pain whenever his feet slipped off the trail. Right after, he bumped into the boy in front of him, who let out a curse.

"Oh yeah? You'll pay for that."

"I didn't mean to! I can't see..."

"I'll open your eyes for you."

On the next round, the boy let himself fall behind, then jabbed the ends of his bundle into Gaitinhas's back, tearing his shirt.

"Cut it out," Gaitinhas groaned. "I'm telling the master."

Without intervening, Zarolho smiled. He even welcomed fights like that, since they made the crew move faster. That's why, when no fights broke out, he'd stir them up himself by putting two or three boys up to it and rewarding them after.

"Once I set this down, I'll break your face!" Gaitinhas threatened. But he dropped his load and didn't swing at the other boy. His bleeding feet sapped his spirit; Zarolho, nearby with a rod in hand, held Gaitinhas's rage in check. He bent down for a moment—to pull out a few thorns—and the master immediately struck his sweaty back.

"Pulling thorns is for nighttime!" And he followed that with a string of insults.

With tears clouding his eyes, Madalena's son couldn't even see the trail. He made his way back to the boat, pushing through thistles sharper than the dry pine needles on the ground.

"Don't cry, Gaitinhas," Guedelhas told him. He'd arrived with other boys to speed up the unloading before the boat got stuck in the mud. "These guys will run out of steam soon. You'll see."

And sure enough, when the sun opened cracks on the dun earth, which was wrinkled like the master's face, and the bundles of firewood beside the kiln numbered in the hundreds, the boys began to slow down. Their feet felt heavy, as if dragging chains, and tears joined the sweat streaming down the pale faces of some of them.

"Can I go drink some water, master?"

"Drink piss! Nobody leaves before quitting time."

The tears were salty. They didn't quench the boys' thirst, nor their helpless despair. Now and then, the rod cracked down on their sluggishness: "Move it!"

But not even fear could spur them on anymore. The heat smothered their spirit; the river was a distant mirage that doubled their thirst.

Guedelhas felt dizzy just seeing water beneath him, so close—and yet so far... *What if I faked a fall?* He moved closer to the woodpile, and when he went to hand over a bundle, he plunged into the filthy water of the inlet, where sewer pipes emptied out.

Some of the boys laughed; others envied their lucky workmate who, pushing away slime and waste with his hands, managed to ease the thirst and heat he felt.

Zarolho approached, fuming. "What kind of joke is this?"

"I fell, master..."

"I'll straighten you out, you rascal."

But when Guedelhas climbed out, he was all filthy and reeking like a sewer rat, so he escaped punishment.

More painful and frantic now, the grind went on, until the Great Factory's whistle, like an alarm bell, sent the boys scattering. While some sprawled face down along the riverbank, others who lived far away ran home as fast as their wobbly legs allowed.

Aching and limping, Gaitinhas headed to the corner of the kiln where he'd left his small bag with bread and olives—but his lunch was gone. He searched around, eyeing the food of his workmates sitting in the shade. Then, staring at the ground, he crouched down too, elbows on his knees and head in his hands.

Caked in mud, Sagui showed up. "Not eating, Gaitinhas?"

"My bag got stolen..."

"Did you check those guys over there?"

"Sure did. But there's a bunch of them eating bread and

olives…"

"Never mind. I'll share with you."

The two of them nibbled on the meager snack. Gaitinhas complained about his friend disappearing for so long.

"They sent me to the *foca*…[49] That hole over there," Sagui explained. "You gotta see it." Then, noticing his friend's feet, he exclaimed, "Whoa! You've got blood all over them. Come wash it off."

They hunkered down among the reeds, sheltering from the sun. Off in the distance, in the workyard, having barely recovered from the toil, Guedelhas was kicking a rag ball around—he still had faith in the club job. Gaitinhas dipped his feet in the river and thought about the pair of boots he'd buy someday.

"How much do boots cost, Sagui?"

His buddy shrugged. "Around thirty *paus*,[50] at least… Why?"

Gaitinhas didn't answer. *Thirty* mil-réis… *I'll never save up that much.* And as his thoughts drifted, he felt a pang for his mother and his school days.

"We work ourselves to death here," he muttered.

"This is nothin' yet. Once they fire up the kiln, that's when you'll really feel the pain."

But he noticed his friend's glum face and added, "It's just until you get used to it, you know?"

"Hmm… I can't stand the tilery much longer."

"I used to say that too, but I always end up back here."

Silence fell. The humidity from the inlet eased their weariness; the calm of the afternoon and the bluish river, looking like a molten strip of the sky, lulled them into drowsiness. Behind them, the tileries and hills had dun and ochre hues that cast a desolate pall. But the two boys only noticed the contrast when they returned to the workyard.

Sluggishly accompanying them were the white horse and the new mule—the one Zé Vicente had bartered for with a few thousand bricks. With kicks and shouts, the crew hitched them to the poles of the mill and the *foca*. And the grind, now even more grueling after a fleeting rest, resumed for beasts and boys alike.

✦ ✦ ✦

AT NIGHT, Gineto's gang gathered at the sporting tavern. It was a squalid dive tucked away in an alley no one dared walk through for fear the air might run out. Only the boys, who were barred from entering other taverns, went there to play at being men: drinking, gambling, and arguing about soccer amid cursing and clouds of smoke.

It was a real find, that little shack of a tavern with its bare tile roof, two tables and long benches, and a wine barrel behind a counter so grimy it even dimmed the posters of famous athletes glued randomly to the walls.

The tavern keeper approached the group, rubbing his hands on a filthy rag. He poured wine, and then, as usual, asked for the latest soccer news, though he'd never played the game.

But the boys brushed him off, absorbed as they were in

Maquineta's story.

"…After the guy slapped me, I decked him and bolted. I was sick of puttin' up with him."

"And now what? You're out of a job."

"I'm gonna join you guys."

"Zarolho's no better than that guy, you know…"

Maquineta struck the back of his own neck hard and, as if arguing with the master himself, he asserted, "No one's gonna yoke this, not even if they kill me."

The others looked on with amazement at their friend who, just two months before, talked about the Great Factory like it was a dream castle. Maquineta seemed older now. And his eyes glinted colder than Gineto's, whenever he stirred up the streets with shouts and fists.

Pirica downed his third glass of wine to cheer up, too. But his woozy head slumped onto the table and he fell asleep.

Gineto chose a partner for a game of *bisca* and, circling back to the tilery talk, declared, "They won't catch me workin' there, no way."

That's why, when he got home, his mother's words were heavy and wet with tears.

"You're living the easy life, son; you don't care about anything. You see the state your father's in… always drunk. And you, who should be the head of the family now…"

"Head of the family?!" Gineto repeated.

He kept mulling over those alluring words, which opened the doors to a new world for him. *Head of the family… No more scoldings from my mom, no more being scorned by men… Drinking at Ramadas tavern, side by side with the Dock Warden…*

Having a girl... He fell asleep late that night, thinking about Rosete. And when the factories' clamour roused the village at eight o'clock, he showed up at Zé Vicente's tilery.

"Hey there!" Zé Vicente said. "Come to spend a few days here, eh?"

"I'll stay till the end, if you give me work."

"Look, I won't put up with any nonsense... One slip-up, and you know what happens..."

"Alright, boss."

He was about to reveal that he was now head of his family, but the master silenced everything with two bellows. The work animals got startled into a trot at the mills; water rushed faster to the clay pits; and even the sun peeked through the clouds to watch the crew's hustle.

A bunch of newcomers, with caps pulled down to their ears and baskets in hand, had stopped in the middle of the workyard, looking lost.

"Hey, country bumpkins!" the others mocked as they laughed.

Gineto understood the naive smiles they gave him and felt sorry for them.

Every year, groups like that would come down from the hills to the tileries. And the crew would hound them with taunts and jeers, just because they wore rustic caps and carried in their eyes the innocence of their places of birth.

"You waitin' for orders? Put your baskets down and go find the master," Gineto advised.

But Zarolho was already on his way over to them.

"What, want me to carry you in my arms?!" he roared.

"Country bumpkins…"

Less fearful than the rest, one of the boys stepped forward and stammered, "We don't know nothin', boss. It's our first time…"

"Just crawled out from under your mothers' skirts, eh?"

Blushing, they shrank back even more, as if admitting the master was right. Then, one by one, they joined the crew feeding bricks into the kiln.

It was a line of boys in constant motion, like an ant trail in the middle of a harvested field. It started at the far end of the workyard where the old pond sparked cravings for cool relief, then snaked between stacks of firewood, and finally disappeared into the kiln's entrance, which could barely fit a grown man.

Right on their first round trip, the newcomers' heels bled, stomped as they were by the bribed feet of Carraça[51] and others of his ilk. The line lost its rhythm and broke apart, and some bricks tumbled from the boys' skinny shoulders when they bumped into each other.

The head master came running, rod held high and curses on his lips.

"Who did this?!"

Carraça spoke up. "They're not rushing, master. Just messing around…"

"That's not true," Coca objected. "He stepped on us."

"Shut up! Move faster and you won't have anyone touching you."

Then, seeing the little boy's shock at the injustice, he barked, "What're you starin' at? Move it! Let's go, move it!"

The shout spread across the tilery, and the mill master echoed it.

Gaitinhas sped up his handcart, which carried bricks stacked on boards that clattered like rattles when the cart was empty. In the workyard, while the stackers unloaded, Madalena's son wiped beads of sweat from his scorching forehead. He was reminded of the toy carts he used to play with in Arturinho's garden. He sighed.

"Out of breath already?" Gineto asked, feeling for him. "If I could, I'd trade places with you."

"Thanks. I can handle it. I'm just thirsty."

"Go over to the pond real quick…"

The master's voice hit them like a rock. "Enough chitchat! Get moving."

Gaitinhas grabbed the cart and headed for the mill. The clay—compressed by a piston and sliced evenly by combs— came out of the moulds in long rectangular slabs, minute by minute.

"Get out… Your turn, boy."

As soon as one cart was loaded up, another took its place. Nearby, Pirica—the clay ball feeder—gritted his teeth as he hurled up the clay balls that Maquineta brought him. His chest was bursting from exhaustion; the endless circling of the scrawny animal, driven by the master's whipping, made him dizzy. Or maybe that was due to the wine he'd downed on an empty stomach that morning.

"Maquineta, ease up on the balls," he whispered.

"What's the point, man? As long as that thing's running…"

And he pointed to the mill's machinery, which he no

longer observed with the curiosity of a budding mechanic. Beyond the inlets, the Great Factory brought back memories of a certain spring dawn, when he'd put a shroud over his childhood dreams. There was the dock where his knack for metalwork had been laid to rest. The sarcastic laughter of the stevedores still echoed in his ears, along with the harsh voice of Má-Cara: *"You slacker! Load him up with more weight…"*

As he relived those memories, he forgot he was now a clay feeder at Zé Vicente's tilery. The mill master noticed the tray was empty and shouted from afar, "Bring more balls, you lazy ox! If I go over there, you'll crap yourself!"

Let him come. He won't be laughing like Má-Cara. Maquineta felt in his pocket for the knife he'd bought from Gineto. A wicked smirk flickered on his coarsely shaped lips. *Let him come…* But then he thought of his mother—for whose sake he endured the toil and insults—and ran off to the *foca*, where Sagui, wearing himself out inside the narrow hole, was powerless to shift the clay that tumbled from the machine. Half a metre below ground level, his hands now brushing his feet, now reaching above his head, he roasted his body inside those walls cracked by the heat, all under the midday sun. He'd turn around every so often, but his spot was always the same, just as the pain stabbing at his lower back like red-hot tongs was always the same. From down there, he couldn't even soothe his eyes on the river's clear waters. He breathed the dust that the white horse kicked up around him and enviously watched the hurried feet of the crew moving in the workyard. Mud and sweat smeared his baby face.

"Maquineta," he groaned. "Ask the master if I can go

relieve myself…"

"Ask him yourself…"

Sagui cursed at him, and he laughed. But after carrying more balls to Pirica, Maquineta jammed the *foca* by getting a rock stuck inside it. Too weak to make the drum's paddles turn, the horse stopped, and Zarolho came running to spur it on with kicks and whipping.

"Why's this thing not moving?" he yelled at Sagui.

"I don't know, master. Maybe something jammed it…"

"So you *do* know. If I find out it was you, I'll thrash you!" And he flailed his arms over the *foca* pit like a vulture looming over its prey.

The mill master came to warn him that the clay was poorly kneaded, since some bricks had already crumbled in the machine. Zarolho then turned his anger on the ditch diggers.

"Don't you know how to use a hoe? You gotta dig deep! The clay pits aren't like the inlets."

"We know how…"

"Then do as I say. And in the mud grounds, you break up the clods properly."

He noticed there was just a trickle of water flowing in the clay pit's sluice and hopped over the flood wall, behind which a boy had hunkered down.

"Taking a nap, eh?" the master said when he saw the boy scramble up in a panic.

"No, sir. I just came to relieve myself."

"Without pulling your pants down, is it? I'm docking half a quarter from your pay—that'll teach you."

Among the reeds, mired in the inlet, another boy held his

breath, fearing Zarolho might sniff him out. But the master turned to hassle Arlindo about the water.

"Keep pulling that lever. The river's not gonna run dry, you know."

"I haven't stopped yet, master."

"Sure, but half-full buckets won't cut it."

Arlindo fell silent. *Even with just one eye, the damn master sees everything.* It was true he wasn't drawing much water, but his arms were already aching. Besides, being alone out there, he tended to forget the tilery was just beyond the wall. A swallow skimmed its black wings over the river in whimsical flight; clouds piled up and then dissolved at the wind's whim; red and white sails in the distance looked like patches sewn onto the landscape. Everything seemed to flee from there, from that scorched patch of land that sprouted only thistles and hardship. And so his thoughts fluttered off too, toward the fields of the Mondego, where Micas, his woman, would be hard at work at that hour.

In the clay pits, as they swung hoes or hauled mud in handbarrows, Arlindo's workmates were grumbling too.

"That bastard of a master thinks he owns the place."

"He's just suckin' up to the boss. I can't wait for the neap tides. At least he doesn't stick his nose in the inlets then."

"The problem is the water hasn't even started to turn yet," the foreman reminded them.

The others fell quiet and, in a burst of anger, drove their hoes into the packed mud.

✦ ✦ ✦

AT LUNCHTIME, after swallowing their last chunk of bread, the boys went for a swim.

They were a bunch of naked, hairless bodies glistening in the sun. All of them skinny, they displayed their bones as they ran and goofed around along the inlets' banks; then they dove in for a first plunge to wash off the sweat. Gineto swam out to the mouth of the inlet, daring the others to catch up; and soon more arms churned the water, which turned murky and viscous.

Fresh from the hills, the newcomers egged on the race with shouts and clapping. Guedelhas urged them. "Come on in, you country bumpkins. The water's great!"

"We dunno how to swim..."

"I'll teach you, pal."

They smiled timidly, and Guedelhas suggested putting on a little show to help them get over their shyness. But Carraça's group was already wading into the inlet—and the others were lining up for battle.

"It's war! It's war!" Gineto hollered the alarm.

Chunks of mud flew through the air; silt rose to the water's surface, smearing everything. Carraça was stuck, with his legs bogged down in the inlet, so he took hit after hit of mud and burst into ridiculous bawls, while the rest of his crew ran away. It was a pathetic cry, and the newcomers savoured every sob.

"Go on, try stepping on our heels now!"

"I'm telling the master..." Carraça blubbered. "You'll pay

for this, I swear."

But when Zarolho called them back to work, he was still naked and filthy on the inlet's edge, looking for his clothes, which Coca had hidden in the reeds.

Then the crew's laughter died down. The sun robbed the freshness the river had given their bodies. Only Zarolho never tired of shouting all afternoon: "Move it! Come on, move it!"

III

BENT OVER, sweat dripping, they spent two days on the task of loading the kiln—brick by brick, row by row, switching from one end to the other so the staggered bricks would later allow the flames to pass evenly, from the arches all the way to the firebrick lining.

Impatient, nibbling at his cigarette, Zé Vicente leaned over the ledge again and again to shout: "Come on! What's the holdup, folks?"

"This is the kind of work you can't see, boss. But we've stacked a fair few rows already…"

"At this rate, it's never reaching the top."

They were thinking the same thing, sick as they were of staring at the same patch of sky that seemed to sit atop the charred walls, where the sun struck dizzying glares.

Still, hours later, as fatigue broke their backs and the kiln workers' mouths panted from being as dry as baked bricks, the kiln was lit. A thick, acrid smoke swirled out through the cracks in the firebricks, enveloping the boys. Harsh coughing fits broke out across the darkened workyard.

"I can't see a thing," Gaitinhas complained, rubbing his eyes.

Gineto seized the chance to sneak off to the inlet. But Zarolho, whose gaze could cut through the darkness, bellowed, "Where's Gineto?"

"Don't know, master."

"And you, what've you been up to? Look at this unpaired brick! You clumsy fool!"

Choking, with his eyes burning, Gaitinhas started flipping the bricks as fast as his trembling, inexperienced hands allowed. Between two gusts of smoke that the wind dragged across the tilery, the boy could see the master's lean, twisted silhouette in the middle of the workyard, like the ghosts Sagui used to go on about.

"First one to finish this stretch gets to take off!" Zarolho shouted.

The crew doubled their efforts, vying with one another. Zé Vicente came over too, to watch those deft hands piling the bricks atop each other in a crisscross pattern. Gaitinhas was coughing and falling behind.

"What's the holdup, boy?"

"This one's no good, boss," the master explained. "He's a total dimwit."

He grabbed the boy's arm and asked, "Don't you know how to count 'em right? One brick down, one empty space—one, two... one, two..."

The boy's eyes were clouded with tears, and his throat was tight with sobs on the verge of breaking loose. No, he didn't know how to count anymore—not in this test, with Zé Vicente as the proctor. He, the best student in his class, was going to flunk. And the master wasn't going to say what Mr. Mesquita had said the previous year: *This boy's going places...*"

In the end, he didn't even make it halfway. His workmates were the ones who'd gone places, as they'd finished the task before time and left, hopping with joy. Still, Zé Vicente tried to cheer him up: "No need to cry over it. You'll win next time."

He stifled his sobs, but the tears still clung to his eyes, red as they were from the firing's black smoke, which was growing thicker and thicker.

Gineto had done well to duck out to the inlet, far from that torment. He searched among the reeds for some fresh excrement, pulled down his pants and squatted to rest. A foul odour filled his nose, but he grinned, thinking of the trick he was about to pull on the master.

And sure enough, Zarolho crept up with his rod raised. "What're you doing there?"

"I came to relieve myself. Look…" He pointed to the waste behind him.

"I don't want any dawdling. Do your business and get moving."

"I'll be right there, master."

Zarolho walked off, and Gineto lingered there a few moments more with his pants still down, chuckling with pride at the stunt he'd come up with and sure that the master would never again dock his pay for time wasted in the inlets. That night, he told his friends about his trick, swearing them to secrecy. Sitting on the kiln's steps, they shattered the tilery's silence with their belly laughs.

They'd gather there on moonlit nights after sipping drinks at the sporting tavern, where the heat was unbearable. They'd play *sete-e-meio*[52] with bets set at half a *tostão,* discuss raids on loquat orchards, and tell stories about the Pine-Puller and the Seven-Headed Beast.

But what really hooked them were the true tales of Ti Alberto, the eldest of the ditch diggers, who'd seen the world.

"Ti Alberto, tell us the one about the ice mountain..."

Without protest, Sagui would cut short whatever old yarn he was spinning. And the ditcher would begin: "Once, on a very foggy day..."

The boys would close their eyes to avoid seeing the stars and the moon.

"... we were out cod fishing, freezing our bones off..."

"Each man in his own boat, right, Ti Alberto?"

"Let him tell it," Gineto would snap.

The ditcher would resume his adventure, and the boys would drift off in their minds to the banks of Newfoundland to battle ice and storms.

Down by the mouth of the kiln, at the bottom of a sloping path clogged with pine branches, the kiln worker would feed the fire, getting his face and chest blackened by the flames that burst from the gaping furnace. Yet the boys, caught in a spell by Ti Alberto's words, would almost shiver. Heat would only come to them later, when the man described Brazil's sun-scorched lands.

On nights like those, the kiln worker wouldn't even bother asking, "Who's up for tossing a bundle of kindling into the back end?" No one would ever go near the mouth of the kiln.

On one occasion, Ti Alberto and the other ditch diggers felt moved by the boys as well. By the inlets, the wind was howling through the reeds and the moon was lost among the clouds. Sagui recalled the stormy night of the floods and told them the story of how Rita Pinta's husband—the ditcher who'd refused to return to his hometown empty-handed—had likely died...

✦ ✦ ✦

IT WAS on a night like that, moonless and starless, that Zarolho came calling for the crew. He knocked on Gineto's door—the boy lived nearby—and startled Maria do Bote.

"Who is it?"

"The tilery master. Tell your son to come stack the bricks—it's raining."

"I'm not going, Mom."

"He'll fire you, you know..."

"I don't care."

He wrapped himself in his blanket so he wouldn't hear his mother's nagging, but her voice, punctuated by his father's drunken snores, still reached his ears.

"I raised my children for nothing. They wouldn't mind seeing me dead..."

"No need to cry. I'm gettin' up."

Still groggy, with crusty eyes, he pulled on his pants and went out.

"Were you waitin' for the sun to come up?" Zarolho grumbled. "Go get the others, quick."

Gineto ran through the deserted streets and roused his friends. Maquineta, however, thought back to the dawn when he'd started at the Great Factory—and didn't leave the house.

"Tell the guy I'm sick."

In the workyard, the master asked if anyone was missing,

but Gineto said no. Under a heavy downpour that was chilling their bodies, still warm from bed, they began covering the bricks. All around, everything was dark. Only the odd flash of lightning lit up the night.

"Aren't we gonna light a fire, master?"

"You can see just fine. Firewood's expensive."

Zarolho's voice boomed across the tilery like the thunder rolling across the sky.

"Hurry up! Cover those piles."

The crew dragged over old tiles and zinc sheets to cover the raw bricks that were already starting to lose their shape under the rain. Every now and then, the boys let out curse words and insults as they bumped into each other in the dark. Groping his way along, Gaitinhas tripped and fell in the mud grounds. Zarolho fell into despair, as the rain wouldn't let up and there wasn't enough covering for so many bricks.

"Bring pine branches! This all needs to be covered, whatever it takes."

And he cursed the bad weather that was ruining the firing batch and the promise of a raise they'd made to him. Zé Vicente's words already spelled a sure rejection: "Just what I needed now. Damned rain!"

"You said it, boss. And in July, too, with all those days of good weather we'd been having… But God willing, we won't have any trouble. The bricks were partly hardened already, except for a few piles over there, which I had the boys cover right away…"

Zé Vicente kept pacing around the workyard, and Zarolho trailed him like a mutt barking at its owner's heels, more out of habit than any expectation of kindness. He wanted to mention his small house, which was deteriorating more and more each winter due to rain, wind, and the humidity from the pond. But Zé Vicente didn't let him beat around the bush.

"If everything's taken care of, send them home."

He adjusted the collar of his overcoat and walked out through the gate. At the master's word, the crew bolted too, splashing water from their rumpled clothes as they ran. As he passed by Zarolho, Coca pointed out, "You know I've been at it from the start, master."

"So what?"

"It's just so you can tally my time."

The master let out a loud laugh.

"Eager for your cut, are you? Go sleep it off and don't pester me, boy."

Meanwhile, the storm had passed. Over the slumbering floodplain, a faint glow was announcing the day.

✦ ✦ ✦

ON OTHER NIGHTS, when the moonlight seemed to pour down the kiln's old, worn-out steps, and the inlets resembled a row of mirrors, the boys would get lost in thought while staring at the stars. The breeze would carry sounds of distant melodies; frogs would croak in the pond's mosses; a shooting star would streak across the sky. And then someone would break the group's silent spell.

"Gaitinhas, sing us a *fadinho*…"

The boy's drawling voice would quiet the frogs and the breeze.

"Denim clothes and a cap
'I'm no-good, or so they say…'"

"Not that one," Maquineta, with a sudden somberness, said one time.

The others protested.

"That one's sweet. Sing it, Gaitinhas."

"But I don't wanna hear it, alright?"

"Who told you you're in charge, pal?" Gineto shot back.

"You aren't either."

"I'm more in charge than you. I lead the gang."

"There are no leaders anymore. It's every man for himself now."

And with that, he walked off.

The others commented on Maquineta's attitude—how he was getting moodier and more short-tempered by the day—but none of them realized that those verses stirred up his sorrow at not wearing a denim outfit like the metalworkers at the Great Factory.

So Gaitinhas's mournful voice still reached his ears:

"Denim clothes and a cap
'I'm no-good, or so they say…'
They're two signs of the creed
Of the crowds that toil away."

Maquineta clapped his hands over his ears and fled in despair.

IV

THE WHITE HORSE died on a sweltering afternoon of hard labour at the mills. His head hung limp between his legs as he sagged in the straps that bound him to the shaft. Zarolho threw two buckets of water over him, thinking it was just a passing heatstroke, and Sagui removed his blinders. But the animal didn't move again.

Only moments before his death, Sagui had ordered, "Turn around, Branquinho."[53] And the horse had reversed the mill's gears like a human would have done. Whenever his friend told him to stop, he immediately understood that mud was overflowing from the *foca*. And when the master would come over to give him a brutal flogging, Branquinho, loyal as ever, never defended his innocence with neighs or kicks.

That's why Sagui wept for him. Zé Vicente mourned the loss of his workhorse too, but only because he didn't have enough money for a replacement—not because he remembered how the old animal had served his father Vicente with the same devotion he'd served him.

Afterward, the master had the horse thrown into the old pond, where it was left to rot amid weeds and sludge, his sores crawling with flies.

The ditch diggers, who washed their clothes there, complained that the pond wasn't a graveyard. Still, no one removed the carcass. Unable to grasp that the horse—all skin and bone, broken—had been their equal in station, the boys even got to making fun of Sagui.

"Did you know? Sagui's dad kicked the bucket..."

"Better him than me."

"Shut up, man. You're gonna make the kid cry..."

The boy would've been the butt of their jokes for days, if another event hadn't stirred the tilery.

That afternoon, Mr. Castro rolled through the gate in a luxury automobile, in the company of the Great Factory's manager and two other gentlemen. Zarolho went over to greet them with a grand show of courtesy and a tip of his hat.

"Mr. Castro, how have you been? I'll send for the boss."

"No, that won't be necessary."

And he led the delegation forward. They climbed the kiln's steps, skirted the pond, and lingered for quite a while by the inlets, near the ditch diggers, whom they didn't even bother to notice.

Just to be safe, Zarolho sent for Zé Vicente, who showed up in a panic, not knowing how to justify his overdue rent payments.

"Greetings, Zé Vicente!"

"Mr. Castro! What brings you here? Such a pleasure..."

He forced his lips to smile while his eyes scanned the other men's faces, trying to guess the purpose of the visit.

"We were just passing through and came to have a look at this place. These tileries must be ancient, no?" inquired one of the anonymous gentlemen.

"My late father used to say they date back to the Moors."

"It's an interesting industry."

"But it's not lucrative anymore. Back in the old days, when we made Portuguese tiles, it was worth the trouble. Now there are more modern methods, other materials…"

He glanced sideways at the Great Factory's manager, who was smiling enigmatically, and fell silent. They walked toward the automobile. In front of the mill, the two gentlemen stopped again to observe the crew at work, and one of them remarked, "Now this is a proper school of labour. Yes, indeed—rather than becoming vagrants, these boys here are being made into men."

Mr. Castro agreed, having forgotten his own youth. And Zé Vicente chimed in with examples of the tileries' educational impact. He sighed for the days of the Monarchy, when even convicts were sent there to serve out long sentences by working from dawn to dusk under the guards' whips.

"And production couldn't keep up with demand back then," he added, hoping to highlight the contrast with current sales. But Mr. Castro cut the conversation short by starting the engine. The car drove off. And Zé Vicente returned to the workyard feeling uneasy and gnawed by suspicions that rumours would confirm a few days later.

"Word's going around that Castro sold the land your tilery's on to the Great Factory."

His heart sank.

"Is that possible?!"

"People are talking three hundred *contos*…"

Seething, he changed clothes in a hurry and headed for the High Farm. *What a crook! To strike a deal like that without so much as offering me an explanation. Oh, but he's going to hear it!*

Yes, he certainly will!

He mentally drafted his opening lines and knocked on the gate. But when Castro, all smiles, asked if he was there to settle his overdue rent, he lost his train of thought and could only stammer, "No, Mr. Castro. I haven't been able to manage it yet... I was hoping to sell a few batches..."

"I'm not chasing you for it, Zé Vicente."

"I appreciate that..."

He regained his composure. This time, he wasn't going to sink into that armchair that dulled both body and mind. A large portrait hanging on the wall unsettled him. He looked away, and suddenly, as if vomiting it out, he brought up the subject.

"What brings me here is the sale of the tilery to the Great Factory. I heard about it..."

"Rumours, obviously."

"... and since I wasn't consulted, given that I'm the land's tenant and own the machinery..."

"Consulted, Zé Vicente?! What business do you have with my affairs? It's my property... I can sell it, or even give it away if I want. Good heavens!"

Faced with his landlord's outburst, Zé Vicente stammered and shook his head repeatedly. His instinct told him that business matters couldn't be settled by force. So he objected meekly. "Yes, that's true. But I've sunk a fair amount of money into that place, as you well know..."

Meanwhile, Mr. Castro had restored his practiced smile to the corner of his mouth and puffed on his cigar with even more disdain. And it was with a touch of condescension that he listened to the tenant speak about how much the machines were worth and the future of his children.

"Just the other day I had the kiln fixed again… It pains me. I practically cut my teeth in that place…"

"Sentimentality, Zé Vicente."

He placed his hand on Zé Vicente's shoulder and, changing his tone, went straight for the kill—like a *matador* in the arena after dominating the bull.

"Listen, Zé Vicente. Obviously, you didn't come here to swindle me, and I have no intention of exploiting you. The tilery's worthless. The machines aren't even good for scrap. In any case, you're free to take them. And as for the sheds, the kiln, and the bunkhouses, I'll pay you their fair value, nothing more."

"And what about the business losses I'll face, Mr. Castro? Yes, the losses…"

"They're offset by the rent you haven't paid."

"What?!…"

The tenant was stunned, but he wasn't beaten just yet.

"That won't do, Mr. Castro! I'll pay the rent. I will pay it!"

"In that case, I'll give you a month's time…"

"Very well. I'll pay you—even if it kills me!"

And he strode back to the tilery, gesturing wildly.

The crew finished work and left; the sun went down. Surrounded by shadows, the tenant lingered there. The evening breeze cooled his fevered mind. Slowly, he began to grasp that he was a castaway adrift in the ocean of life. He took stock of his own strength—and felt powerless to reach shore and set a new course. Now, at last, he saw clearly the magnitude of the

Great Factory and the shadow it cast over the tilery. The dark silhouette of the smokestack seemed to detach itself, ready to come crush him beneath the rubble of the kiln that had once belonged to his father and that he'd always believed was his.

Across the inlet, lamps flickered and engines rumbled. No, it was no use trying to raise the money—and where would he even get it?—because the law of the survival of the fittest would prevail sooner or later. It was an unfair law, perhaps, but a law nonetheless. Mr. Castro was right. That which does not renew itself is doomed. And he had never modernized the tilery. Even the white horse from the mill had collapsed from old age and now lay rotting in the pond that had once been a source of clay.

He too had been broken, and would soon end up in the mass grave of the destitute. His children would abandon their studies and become grunts at the Great Factory or rookies at the tilery owned by Meneses, the magnate, while he'd be left with nothing but the small shop that went with the business.

But he couldn't allow that. He'd give his children a better future, even if he had to starve, even if he had to toil across hills and valleys. A shaft of moonlight struck his face full on, scattering the shadows around him. In his darkest hour, he too thought he could make out a light at the end of the tunnel. He'd ask Castro for an advance on the buildings, as the landlord had proposed, and run the tilery full tilt until October, churning out batch after batch. And with the profits from that, he'd expand the shop and his business...

It was to these thoughts that Zé Vicente fell asleep that night.

✦ ✦ ✦

WHEN THE BOYS learned about the sale, they figured it was a *day of light*—as the few off days at the tileries were once called. Smiles spread across every face, and comments passed from group to group. Maquineta shed his surly, feral look. And after lunch, Pirica showed up cheerfully drunk, which earned him a punishment: no work and no pay that afternoon.

Zarolho threatened to fire the whole crew, because the *foca* had jammed due to carelessness, and out on the yard, the bricks weren't being flipped with the proper diligence. Here and there, there was chatter.

"We'll finally get jobs at the Great Factory."

"Wow! This place might not even last a month. Hey, Maquineta! This time you're buying those coveralls…"

"But has the tilery really been sold?" Guedelhas asked.

"Of course it has."

"That means we already work for the factory."

"That's right!"

Their excitement burst into jumps and shoves, until Zarolho's rod put an end to it.

The joy grew even stronger in the late afternoon, at the end of work. "Let's go hit the grapes, fellas!" one of them shouted.

Like a flock of sparrows, the crew raided the valley, which was now one big, bountiful orchard, even though the loquat and cherry trees had already been severely stripped by then. But it was the grapes that sated the boys' hunger at any hour. People even said that Antunes never managed to harvest his old, unwalled vineyard before the boys got to it.

Gineto, however, preferred the lush estates of Castro and others, where they had choice grapes that were sweet as honey. He put on an old coat, stolen from his father, that hung down to his knees, and climbed the wall while the others waited by the roadside.

"Mr. Miguel, please give me a bunch of grapes..." he called out from his perch.

He waited, then pleaded again, "Mr. Miguel..."

No one answered. The silence and the closed doors of the mansion suggested the caretaker was either far off or not inside the estate at all. Sagui reported that the big dog was also locked up in the garden.

They jumped into the vineyard. Gineto darted between the vines, his coat brushing against them as he searched for muscat grapes. He ate some first, then started stuffing the folds of his shirt with them, keeping the coat empty so it wouldn't hamper his movements.

By the wall, his friends were plucking grapes and laughing. Some were sitting, others were squatting, but all of them were at ease, as if the estate belonged to them. That day, they felt like they owned the world. Even Gaitinhas, who was always so timid, stretched out on the damp grass under the vines, listening to the songs of crickets and cicadas as his whole body bathed in the soft peace that filled the air together with the scent of fruits and flowers. He wanted to sleep, to dream...

Suddenly, the rustle of footsteps startled the gang, and they scattered like a litter of rabbits, with the caretaker bellowing after them, "Ah, you thieves! Sons of the devil!"

Caught off guard by the unexpected attack, the boys tried in vain to scramble over the wall. Despite being hidden under the leaves, Gaitinhas was about to be caught when Gineto stepped in, challenging the caretaker, who rasped, "You're not getting away this time, you little bastard!"

He grabbed for Gineto's coat, which came off in his hands, and immediately got a bunch of grapes thrown in his face. Gineto kept taunting him, dodging and weaving between the vines to give Gaitinhas and the others time to escape. And when he found himself alone in the vineyard, he suddenly crouched down and bolted after the others, who asked him afterwards, "Where's your coat, Gineto?"

"The guy's got it. If it weren't so baggy, I'd be done for too."

He laughed and added, "But he's gonna pay for it, big time…"

✦ ✦ ✦

AFTER THE INITIAL days of joy following the sale of the tilery came disillusionment. The grind continued, now harder and more pressing, under a dizzying heat. It was August, and the sun on the boys' skin felt like embers fanned by the wind. In the workyard and at the mills, Zé Vicente—sleeves rolled up and pine branch in hand—urged the crew on and whipped the animals, who wouldn't even trot because they were underfed and weak.

He'd bought another one. Mr. Castro's payout had also covered five boatloads of firewood, two of which were already stacked beside the kiln. In the main inlet, the choppy river waters at high tide now reflected the slender silhouettes of boats waiting to be loaded with bricks. That's why Zé Vicente was rushing about from one end of the tilery to the other, harassing the masters.

"How's that batch coming?"

"Still cooling, boss. Can't be taken out for another twenty-four hours."

"The hell it can't! Just cut the bricks and spare me the theory."

The men unsealed the kiln, removing the red-hot firebrick covering. Clouds of dust and smoke rose up—it was a whitish, salty dust that seeped into the kiln workers' clothes and skin, stinging their eyes and eating away at their shirts.

They shoveled earth over the layer of powder covering the smoldering bricks, then staggered down the kiln steps like they were drunk. One of them, feeling dizzy from the smoke, slipped and fell off the edge onto a pile of shards, leading him to protest against the kiln's lack of a guardrail.

"That's not right, Mr. Vicente. If I'd gotten hurt…"

"If you'd gotten hurt, the insurance would cover it. Couldn't you see the steps? You think I'm fool enough to spend money fixing up something that belongs to someone else now?"

And after lunch, grumbling with fury because the kiln was no longer his, he ordered the crew to load the boats.

Some boys showed up wearing old, brimless caps or large hats which they had borrowed from relatives or dug out of the trash. Guedelhas turned an old sock from a rag ball into a cap that barely covered his unruly hair. But others, like Gaitinhas, joined the line of loaders bareheaded.

"Aren't you gonna cover your ears, Gaitinhas? You're in for it," his friends told him.

"I've got nothing to cover them with…"

"Grab some tile shards to pad your shoulders with. Quick!"

Gaitinhas stepped out of the line, but the master shoved him back into place.

"Where do you think you're going?" And without waiting for an answer, he commanded, "Anyone with shoes on, jump into the kiln."

None of the boys moved. Each started eyeing the others' feet, and Sagui whispered to Gaitinhas, "So, where's your boots?"

"Haven't bought 'em yet. I've only saved up nine *milréis…*"

The master shouted again, "Didn't you hear me? Bunch of slackers!"

"We're all barefoot. We can't even scrape together enough money for food…"

"Oh, is that so? You, Maquineta, get in the kiln. You too… And you as well. Get moving."

They climbed the rough stone steps that had a flimsy handrail made from old poles on one side for protection.

From the top of the kiln, the air seemed to shimmer, stirred as it was by blasts of heat rising off the bricks. And from the whole tilery—ochre-coloured and cracked, with clumps of dried thistles scattered about and sheds crumbling from age and neglect—rose the smell of sweat built up over generations of workers.

The afternoon's swelter dulled their bodies, but the master

had the line moving in an instant, under Zé Vicente's stern gaze.

"Move up front, boy!"

Maquineta stepped onto the rows of bricks, then immediately jumped back out of the kiln, grumbling, "No one can take it when they're this hot. I got burned already..."

Even though they were wearing shoes, the kiln workers backed up the boy's remarks.

"They haven't cooled for twenty-four hours yet, boss..."

"To hell with that! You lot can't take it? Well, I can."

Zé Vicente grabbed a scorching brick, gritting his teeth to keep from letting out a curse. It burned, no doubt about it, but neither he nor the boats could wait any longer. He needed money at all costs, before the Great Factory took over the land. He remembered the words he'd spoken on his way out of the estate: *"Even if it kills me, Mr. Castro."* Well then, let it kill them all for all he cared, but they'd unload the kiln that afternoon.

"Grab that, boy!"

Gaitinhas shouldered the load, but then let it fall, overcome by the searing heat that pierced through his shirt and burned his shoulders and ears. A shove from the master brought tears of rage to his eyes.

"Bunch of sissies! You want the boss to do your job for you? Any of you who can't take it, you're out!"

The kiln workers and the boys got to unloading the kiln: the men stacked bricks, while the boys piled five of them at a time on each others' shoulders. Zarolho's shouts drowned out both curses and complaints; beads of sweat disguised tears they couldn't hold back.

"Get in there! Move up front, Coca."

Hopping on his good leg as he scraped the other against the edge of the stone steps, Coca went up and down without falling behind. The hardest part for him was crossing the inlet to the boat, over the narrow plank that wobbled under the boys' hurried steps.

Up front, Gaitinhas was crying. He'd shielded his shoulders with two tile shards, like he'd seen the others do; but he had no hat to protect his ears, which were already red with burns from the bricks. The muddy water of the inlet, gradually drained by the ebbing tide, only sharpened his thirst. *If only Zarolho would let me go relieve myself...* He'd wet his lips and sores, and rest for a moment, squatting over someone else's waste as Gineto had taught them.

He approached the master and whimpered, "Can I go to the inlet?"

"No! Nobody leaves here."

But he saw so much anguish in Gaitinhas's face that he relented. "Go on, then. But make it quick, you hear?"

Maquineta also got away from the kiln, as he could no longer bear the heat on his scorched feet. He dipped them in the river and stretched out along the bank on a bed of marsh grass. He wanted to fall asleep like that, gazing up at the scraps of clouds seemingly glued to the sky, oblivious to time, to the tilery, to everything... To let his thoughts drift like that black-sailed flatboat in the distance... And maybe dream of a job he'd never have, in some wonderful workshop, without men like Má-Cara.

But the sound of footsteps in the inlet made him spring to his feet. It was the master, who had noticed his absence.

"Is this how you earn your day's pay? You loafer!"

"I came to wash my feet—they're all burned. You want me to end up disabled, do you?"

Zarolho didn't forgive escapes to the inlet, and even less so allusions to his condition, however vague they might be. His one good eye bulged even more, and he stepped toward Maquineta.

"Still talking back, you little pest?"

"Don't touch me, or I'll report you. You can't hit people."

"I can't, huh? I'll show you if I can't."

Maquineta backed away toward the inlet's far end, which was slippery and tangled with sedges and weeds, making dodging and running impossible there. He searched his pocket for his knife, but couldn't find it. Zarolho seemed even taller to him now, stomping over grass and clumps of earth with his fearsome boots, ready to crush him, too. So, in desperation, Maquineta dove headfirst into the river.

When he surfaced, he still managed to hurl insults for the man to hear. But the current began to pull him, and he realized he wasn't much of a swimmer. He gauged the distance to shore. *A dozen strokes… and I'll make it,* he thought. The inlet was wider in comparison, and he'd already crossed it twice under the watchful eye of Gineto, his swimming instructor. He fought the current, thrashing his arms vigorously, but doing so wore him out quickly. Panic hit him, and a gulp of water made breathing difficult. The river seemed vaster now, the tilery farther away. *Am I going to drown? No. If I shout, my friends will come save me.* He shouted—and swallowed more water. In the swirling chaos of the current and his anxious thoughts, an idea rose to the surface of his mind: *Keep the body flat, and float.* The thought wasn't his own. It was Gineto's voice from back at the inlet, saying, *"Float, buddy, and you won't sink. Just float..."*

Instinctively, he let himself float. And shortly after, when his body bumped against the pier of the Great Factory, he still had the strength to grab onto one of the pilings like a desperate castaway.

Meanwhile, Zarolho had returned to the kiln, where the boys were cursing the bricks, which were hot as ever. One of the boats, loaded to the brim, had already opened its sails to the wind. The sun was leaving the tilery to hide behind the hills, where windmill sails looked like they were waving at the boys from those parts. But the hustle and bustle wouldn't let up.

With his shirt untucked from his pants and wobbling like a rag doll, Coca forgot about the sweat and burns, and started complaining about his lame leg, which could barely carry him up the steps now.

"I wish we could unload straight from the mouth of the kiln already."

"What for, buddy? The lower you go, the hotter the bricks," Sagui explained.

"I don't care. It's like there's more steps to climb now."

"Well, it'll be six o'clock soon..."

"Six? But I heard the factory whistle just now..."

The boys listened intently, but the wind, which had stirred up swirls of dust across the workyard, didn't carry the tower clock's chimes to them. The hustle and bustle went on. And Carraça's bribed feet kept stepping on the heels of the boys ahead of him.

Falling victim to that lousy workmate, Coca lost his balance on the boat's plank, fell into the inlet, and started sobbing as he lay there all covered in mud.

Gineto rushed over to help him up.

"Who pushed you, Coca? Tell me, and I'll bust him up."

When he learned it was Carraça, Gineto lunged at him in a rage, hitting him again and again, until Zé Vicente broke them apart.

"What kind of disrespect is this?! Gineto, get to the *foca!* And if I catch you at it again, you won't set foot in here anymore."

"He started it."

"Hush! I want no fighting here."

"Yeah, right… As if the master doesn't smack us around plenty…"

"Well, I haven't seen any of that. And the master… is the master."

Grumbling, Gineto walked away. And the grind continued until the sun vanished behind the hills, because with all the commotion, the crew hadn't paid any mind to the tower clock.

V

SEPTEMBER. The sun still shines in the last days of summer, but the wind—ruffling the clumps of sedge like it once ruffled the boys' shaggy hair—is colder and sharper.

At the tilery, there lingers a distressing air of abandonment, like in those deserted houses that still hold within their bare rooms some useless relic—a broken chair, perhaps—left behind by their last occupants.

The wrecking crew from the Great Factory left only the kiln's gutted walls amid the rubble. Standing upright in the workyard now littered with debris, they're a reminder of prosperous times and unending toil. Thistles are slowly claiming the ground where children's feet once trod, and a frog has already taken over the shadowy puddle formed by the rain at the base of the slope, where the mouth of the kiln looks like a monster's gaping maw.

Zé Vicente only ever returned there once—to haul off the machines and other property, and to pay the workers—after that night when fire turned the woodpiles, along with his last hopes, to ash.

No one ever figured out how it had started. The kiln was out, and before going to bed, the master had made his usual round of the tilery and seen no one. But soon after, the flames lit the night brighter than the moonlight. Then came the firefighters and the crew, in a frenzy; but drawing water from the pond did no good. That was when Zé Vicente began weeping like a child. And the tilery boys, still children themselves, were moved by it.

Only Maquineta remained impassive, his thick lips barely holding back a strange smile.

"Don't you feel bad?" Gaitinhas asked him.

He shrugged and muttered through his teeth, "This way, we'll get into the Great Factory faster..."

But Maquineta's prediction didn't come true. He and the others hung around the tilery and the factory gates for over a week, but no one called for them. And at the other tileries, not even the ditch diggers were let in, despite the trembling voices with which they pleaded.

After settling debts at the shop and the bakery, the foreman buys tickets for the night train that's running late. The others sit on the station benches under dim lighting and, without words or gestures of contentment, wait for the journey back home.

Arlindo comes to say goodbye to them, feeling as sad as they do.

"So you're stayin' after all?"

With his gaze fixed on the worn tiles of the platform, he nods.

"Please tell Micas that next year..."

The rest of his words dry up in his throat. His eyes hold back tears that, in the darkness of night, can only be seen when the train's headlight reflects off the station's windowpanes.

His companions set down their bags, full of clothes and dreams, in the third-class carriage and come to the window to wave goodbye. The train huffs and departs. And Arlindo stands frozen there, all alone, listening to that same old drone: *"Pouca terra… pouca terra…"*

❋ ❋ ❋

THE TILERY is silent and deserted, and the wind whistles through the reeds in the pitch-black inlets. There isn't a single star in the sky. The dim lights of the flatboats in the distance only deepen the night.

But Gineto isn't afraid. Twice already he's crossed the inlet, mud up to his knees, to steal coal from the Great Factory. The fairgrounds are already being set up in the village square—and he wants to see Rosete again at the shooting stall; he wants to buy kisses from her with money he never managed to save up at the tilery.

So again he crosses the inlet, now brimming with water; then he crawls and dashes toward the coal pile, hurriedly stuffing his sack while keeping alert for sounds and beams of light. But the machines drown out the footsteps of the guards, and the darkness conceals them. When he tries to flee, it's already too late, as he finds himself confronted by men as quick and powerful as Rex, the big dog from the High Farm.

Captured and bound, Gineto sleeps at the post of the Republican Guard after a summary interrogation. Sleeps…? No—he's plotting escapes and thinking his friends will come rescue him, like on that stormy night when the *Boa Sorte* foundered. They won't let their leader stay there, far from the streets where kids play and mess around in, far from the orchards heavy with fruit. He has grand plans for the gang, which until now had done nothing more than steal a few sacks of oranges during the previous winter.

But his friends don't come, and his mother's tears can't undo the testimony of the guards, the caretakers, and the Dock Warden, who bears an indelible scar on his arm left by Gineto's pocketknife...

Days roll by, all alike; autumn arrives, riding the wind. And Gineto still holds the same faith he had when he first entered prison.

In his cell, he hears horses galloping and the clamour of a crowd cutting through the distant, muddled whisper of music, gunshots, and voices... It's the Fair. Gineto takes heart, believing his friends will come for him on this day of celebration, bringing Rosete along. He presses his face to the bars, waiting for his return to freedom.

Just below his window, a voice is singing a song he heard one afternoon atop Mirante. So he shouts, "Gaitinhas! I'm here, Gaitinhas!"

But the voice fades. Gaitinhas, the singer, is off to roam the world alongside Sagui to search for his father. And when he finds him, he'll come back to set Gineto free and send those tilery kids to school—those boys who look like men yet never got to be children.

- The End

Translator's Notes

1   *Master*—From the Portuguese *mestre*. In Portuguese industrial and craft contexts of this era, a *mestre* was both the person in charge of a workplace or operation (similar to a foreman) and a skilled craftsperson with extensive practical knowledge. The English term "master" has been chosen to retain both the sense of authority and craft expertise inherent in the original.

2   *Gineto*—A nickname meaning "genet", which is a small carnivorous mammal found in Portugal. Similar to a raccoon in North American culture, the genet has a reputation as a clever, mischievous creature. The nickname captures the character's wildness and tendency to live outside conventional society.

3   *Sagui*— A nickname referring to small monkeys (marmosets and tamarins) native to Central and South America, reflecting the character's small, scrawny build.

4   *Malesso*— A nickname referring to a bull of "bad blood" or, regionally, a scoundrel or rogue, suggesting a difficult or problematic nature, but also carrying connotations of misfortune.

5   *Guedelhas*— A nickname indicating long, unkempt hair.

6   *Mirante*—A term meaning "lookout"—a high vantage point that provides a wide view of the surrounding landscape. Used throughout the novel as a place name for the lookout point at the top of the hill, from which the alley leading up to it takes its name.

7   *Ti*—A Portuguese form of address derived from *tio/tia* (uncle/aunt), commonly used in rural areas for older men and women—even if they're not actual relatives—conveying respect and familiarity.

8   *Arturinho*—A diminutive of Artur (Arthur). Diminutives are widely used in Portuguese everyday speech, conveying smallness (literal or figurative), affection or familiarity, but also, depending on context and tone, disdain, sarcasm, or pity.

9   *Maquineta*—Diminutive of *máquina* (machine), meaning "gadget".

A nickname indicating the character's fascination with machinery.

10 *Gaitinhas*—Plural diminutive of *gaita* (a wind instrument like a flute or whistle). A nickname referring to the character's love of music and musical instruments.

11 *Tom Mix*—Thomas Edwin Mix (1880–1940) was an American film actor and one of Hollywood's first great stars in the Western genre. A household name at the time, his popularity made him a cultural icon well beyond the United States.

12 *Tostões*—Plural of *tostão,* a colloquial term for 10 *centavos* (one-tenth of an *escudo,* Portugal's official currency at the time of the novel's publication), generally used colloquially for small sums. Here, 'ten tostões' equals 1 escudo, a modest amount for a carousel ride and a small but significant amount for a boy like Gineto.

13 *queijadas*—Traditional Portuguese small tarts made with fresh cheese, eggs, and sugar. A popular sweet often sold at fairs and bakeries.

14 *mil-réis*—Literally "thousand *réis*". A monetary unit from Portugal's previous currency system (the *real,* plural *réis*), equivalent to one *escudo.* The term remained in common use even after the *escudo* was introduced in 1911.

15 *miombas*—Plural of *miomba,* a traditional Portuguese sandwich made with slices of pork or beef, predating the now more common *prego* and *bifana* sandwiches.

16 *Malacara*—A traditional name for a horse with a white blaze extending from the forehead down to the chest. The name comes from Spanish *mala cara* (mean face). Notably, a famous horse named Malacara became legendary for making an impressive jump to save its rider's life in 1884 Patagonia—the likely explanation as to why Gineto chooses a Spanish name for his fantasy horse that vaults over obstacles.

17 *Manel*—A colloquial short form of Manuel, commonly used as a familiar way to address someone with this name in Portuguese.

18 *Coca*—A nickname likely referring to the character's physical disability. In Portuguese, "coca" can mean physical ailment or pain (regional usage), which would fit the character's lame leg.

19 *Pirica*—A family nickname, shared with his uncle Zé Pirica, a boat

skipper. Family nicknames in Portuguese culture often have origins that become obscure over time and may not relate to standard dictionary definitions.

20 *Maria do Bote*—Literally "Maria of the Boat". A common Portuguese naming convention where a person's name is followed by a descriptor— often tied to their occupation, origin, or a defining trait. In this case, *"do Bote"* (of the boat) refers to her husband Manuel's association with his small vessel. In traditional Portuguese culture, wives often took on their husband's occupational or descriptive identifier.

21 *Costa Ourives*—Literally "Costa, the Jeweller". Following the Portuguese naming convention, the surname Costa is combined with *ourives* (jeweller) to identify him by his profession. In Portuguese, it's common to refer to tradespeople by pairing their name with their occupation—especially in small towns or working-class settings.

22 *Chico* —A colloquial short form of Francisco (Francis), Gineto's given name.

23 *aguardente*—"Firewater" or *aguardente* (lit. Burning water) is a traditional Portuguese fruit brandy. It's also sometimes used as a more general term for strong alcoholic beverages, especially moonshine or whiskey.

24 *Boa Sorte*—Portuguese for "Good Luck". A common name for small boats, reflecting a wish for safe voyages.

25 *fadinho*—A diminutive of *fado*, Portugal's traditional song style, often expressing longing or melancholy.

26 *Rosa Coxa*—Literally "Rosa, the Lame". Rosa is a woman's name meaning "rose", while *coxa* means "lame" or "limp". The text establishes a contrast between her beauty (like a rose) and her physical disability, which ultimately defined how others perceived her.

27 *Montepio*—Founded in 1840, Montepio was a mutual aid society in Portugal that provided members with social protection, such as pensions and support during illness or death.

28 *escudos*—Plural of *escudo*, Portugal's official currency from 1911 to 2002. The *escudo* replaced the *real* at a rate of 1 *escudo* = 1,000 *réis* (or 1 *mil-réis*).

29 *Glass shards*—Broken glass fixed along the tops of walls, a traditional

security measure in Portugal and other parts of Europe to deter intruders.

30 *Henri-Frédéric Amiel (1821–1881)*—a Swiss philosopher, poet, and critic, best known for his introspective *Journal Intime,* in which he reflects on the self, nature, and the relationship between inner life and the outer world. The quote referenced aligns with his frequent meditations on how external landscapes mirror emotional states.

31 *contos*—Plural of *conto,* a monetary unit equal to 1,000 *escudos.* Large sums in *contos* indicated significant wealth, typically associated with landowners and industrialists. *Related notes: 12, 14, 27, 48 (currency)*

32 *Estoril*—A coastal town west of Lisbon, historically associated with wealth, aristocracy, and leisure. In the mid-20th century, owning a mansion in Estoril was a clear sign of elite status.

33 *Toino*—A colloquial short form of the Portuguese male name *António* (Anthony), used more commonly in rural areas.

34 *Antoino*—Another colloquial variant of *António* (Anthony).

35 *mistake the cloud for Juno*—A reference to Greek mythology where Ixion mistook a cloud shaped by Zeus for Hera, queen of the gods. The idiom uses her Roman name Juno, reflecting the Latin roots of Portuguese. It means mistaking appearance for reality or exaggerating a situation.

36 *clay pots on windmill sails*—Traditional Portuguese windmills often had unglazed clay pots attached to their sails. These pots, known as *búzios* or *jarras,* were carefully tuned to specific musical notes and served both practical and aesthetic purposes. The sounds they produced as wind passed through them helped millers gauge wind conditions while creating a distinctive soundscape in rural Portugal.

37 *Tonecas*—An informal diminutive of *"António"* (Anthony), commonly used in Portuguese for children.

38 *King of the Cowboys*—A nickname for American actor Roy Rogers (1911-1998), who starred in the 1943 Western film *King of the Cowboys* and numerous other films and TV shows where he typically played heroic characters who fought outlaws and delivered frontier justice. Popular in the 1940s and 1950s, Rogers also gained a following in Portugal through his films and comic books.

39 *bisca*—A popular Portuguese variant of a trick-taking card game of Italian origin, played with a 40-card deck.

40 *Macacoi*—A play on "McCoy", using *macaco* (monkey), showing how foreign names were sometimes humorously adapted. This refers to Tim McCoy (1891-1978), a popular American Western film star of the silent and early sound era.

41 *Fearless Rider*—In the original Portuguese, "Cavaleiro sem Medo". This was likely a localized title for one of Tim McCoy's westerns from the 1930s, possibly *Bulldog Courage* (1935), which was released internationally under various names. Such titles were often loosely adapted or reinvented for local audiences, and the author may have blended elements from multiple films.

42 *campino*—A bull herder, particularly in the Ribatejo region of Portugal, known for their traditional and distinctive clothing including a short smock or jacket.

43 *Má-Cara*—Literally "mean face". The nickname of the factory foreman whose real name is Enriques.

44 *Anriques*—Maquineta's misspelling of Enriques (Má-Cara). The author's deliberate alteration alludes to Maquineta's illiteracy--he left school in the second grade and could not read or write.

45 *Mazzantini*—This likely refers to Luis Mazzantini (1856-1926), a famous Spanish bullfighter known for his sophisticated, dandy-like fashion sense.

46 *pouca terra, pouca terra...*—Portuguese onomatopoeia for the rhythmic sound of train wheels on tracks. Literally "little land" or "not enough land", the expression reflects the workers' landless condition—their lack of property forces them into seasonal migration. The author uses this sound-meaning connection to suggest the train itself is commenting on their predicament, with its mechanical rhythm mocking their economic situation.

47 *Mondego*—The Mondego is a major river in central Portugal, often symbolic of home and longing in Portuguese literature.

48 *Zarolho*—Literally "one-eyed". The nickname of the head master at Zé Vicente's tilery whose real name is Felipe.

49 *foca*—A regional term for "hole", referring to an animal-powered clay

processing device with a below-ground pit where clay is worked.

50 *paus*—Literally "sticks". A slang term for *escudos*.

51 *Carraça*—A nickname meaning "tick" (the parasitic arachnid), suggesting someone who harasses other people.

52 *sete-e-meio*—Literally "seven and a half". A card game similar to blackjack.

53 *Branquinho*—A diminutive of *branco* (white). The affectionate name for the white workhorse that powers machines at Zé Vicente's tilery.

ABOUT THE AUTHOR

SOEIRO PEREIRA GOMES (1909–1949) was a Portuguese writer and militant communist, best known as one of the foremost voices of Portuguese neorealism. Born in Gestaçô, Baião, he studied agricultural engineering at the University of Coimbra before working as a technician at a cement factory in Alhandra. His experiences among industrial and rural workers shaped both his political engagement and his literary output.

A committed member of the Portuguese Communist Party, Pereira Gomes used literature as a tool for social critique, exposing the harsh realities of exploitation and inequality under Portugal's Estado Novo dictatorship. His best-known novel, *Esteiros* (1941), depicts the struggles of working-class children forced into labour, becoming a cornerstone of neorealist literature. Another important work, *Engrenagem* (published posthumously in 1951), examines the mechanisms of oppression within capitalist society.

Persecuted for his political activism, he lived much of his later life in secrecy, suffering from poor health. He died prematurely in 1949, at just 40 years old. Despite his brief career, Soeiro Pereira Gomes remains a central figure in Portuguese literature, remembered both for his artistic contribution and for his unwavering commitment to social justice.

ABOUT THE TRANSLATOR

TIAGO SILVA is a literary and audiovisual translator with extensive experience translating from English into Portuguese since 2016. He has worked with a range of international platforms, specializing in the adaptation of cultural content, films, series, and documentaries. His fluency in English, combined with a keen sensitivity to the Portuguese language, allows him to convey both the meaning and tone of the original texts with precision and fluidity. He is currently translating *Esteiros* by Soeiro Pereira Gomes into English, helping to bring this landmark work of Portuguese neorealism to a broader international audience.

www.ingramcontent.com/pod-product-compliance
Lightning Source LLC
Chambersburg PA
CBHW030035030726
47500CB00001B/111